Fool Me Once

Robyn C Rye

Published by robyncrye, 2024.

Copyright © 2024 by Robyn C Rye

All rights reserved. No part of this publication may be reproduced, distributed or transmitted in any form or by any means without the publisher's prior written permission except as permitted by copyright law.

This book is a work of fiction. Names, characters, places and incidents are a product of the author's imagination. Any resemblance to actual people, living or dead, or businesses, companies, events, institutions or locales is entirely coincidental.

Also by Robyn C Rye

Farnsworth Sisters
Marrying a Rogue
Rescuing Hannah

The Buckingham Sisters
Lady Maggie's Challenge
Layla's Unwanted Husband

The Evans Family
Sometimes Love is not Enough
Still the One
Moving Forward

Standalone
One More Chance
Lady Jayne's Reputation
Third Time's the Charm
Can't Stop Loving You

The Marriage Scam
An Unlikely Match
Searching For You
The Unexpected Suitor
The Lady and the Duke
Starting Over
An Unforgettable Stranger
The Duke's Revenge
The Temporary Wife
Against The Odds
Betrayed
No Good Turn Goes Unpunished
Lady Eloise's Soldier
Lillian's Forbidden Beau
Remember Me
Always Second Best
When One Door Closes
Coming Home to You
Chasing Shadows
Fool Me Once
Deserting Lady Audrey
My Unlikely Saviour
Lies and Deception
A New Beginning
Julia's Second Chance
The Hidden Enemy
The Maiden's Redemption
Miss Elizabeth's Season

Table of Contents

AUTHOR'S MESSAGE

As a reader, you may wonder why some words seem misspelt, but as an Australian writer, I use the spelling of terms in English rather than the American style. So, no! I am not a poor speller; I have used the spell check with an Australian slant.

I loved recounting Amy's story and hope you enjoyed the unfolding story of the trials and successes they endured.

If you liked the book and have a minute to spare, I would appreciate a short review on the page or site where you bought the book. Your help in spreading the word is appreciated. Reviews from readers like you make a massive difference in helping new readers find stories like *Fool Me Once.*

ROBYN RYE@ GOODREADS.com
Robyncrye.author@gmail.com

PROLOGUE

Four years earlier

"Come for a walk with me, Amy. We need to talk."

My boyfriend of three months never exercised without a damn good reason. Lucas's suggestion of a walk and the need to talk sent warning signals from my brain to my tummy.

"Ah, can't we talk here?"

"Come on, lazybones. A walk will clear my head, and the stuff I need to say is important."

I grabbed my tote bag as I headed for the door.

As we walked, I waited with anticipation as Lucas sorted his thoughts. My mind went blank when he linked his fingers through mine and slightly squeezed.

"Okay, here goes. We have been together for three months, and we work well together. I love spending time with you, and I find you sexy as hell. It's too soon to know if what we have is for forever, but even if it's not, we can help each other achieve our goals."

Lucas glanced at her and raised his eyebrows.

"How am I doing so far?"

"Great, except I have no idea where you are going with this."

"You want to be a vet, and I want to be a doctor. We could both go to uni, wrack up enormous debts, and spend the rest of our lives paying back student loans. I want to make a suggestion that might sound unorthodox, but I believe it will work. Are you game to listen to my proposal?"

"Any suggestion you can make that can cut our debts is worth hearing."

"If we move in together, we will drop one rent. Let's face it; we spend so much time together that living together makes sense."

"Okay, I agree. But I hate to point out that living together won't get us debt-free unless you pay heaps of rent on your place."

"Now comes the tricky part. Let's sit at the picnic table under the tree, and I can share my idea with you."

Once they took their seats, Lucas took hold of Amy's hands.

"If one of us works and pays for the other person's fees, then after graduation, we reverse the set-up, and we will both end up with the careers we want. Our debts will be minimal compared to most students' full rates."

"Your suggestion makes sense, but how do we decide who studies first? Do you want to flip a coin?"

"Could we look at who will earn more money in their career first?"

"As a doctor, you will find a job within months of graduating. Even if you secure a job in another town, I should be able to do lots of the non-practical stuff online and then go wherever my placements put me."

"Are you happy being the one who waits?"

"No, but I can see the logic in the plan. Promise me you won't swan off with your doctor's certificate and leave me in the dust."

Lucas wrapped his arms around Amy.

"Sweetheart, that's a promise."

The next few weeks kept Amy and Lucas busy. Not only did they have to move Lucas's belongings to Amy's flat, but they also needed to dispose of excess furniture and wrap up the lease on Lucas' rooms. Amy found it bizarre to share her home with another person. It still felt weird when she walked into a room, and someone else was there. She hoped that the relationship between her and Lucas was for good. While Lucas investigated courses, book hire, and fees, Amy hunted for employment. She worked as a casual barmaid, but casual work meant that her hours were erratic. Should she ask to work full-time?

If her boss guaranteed her hours, that might help her get a second job. With the details of this agreement running through her head, Amy felt a moment of trepidation. She and Lucas had known each other for three months; moving in together was always on the cards, but she had niggling doubts about the plan but pushed aside the worry and moved forward with their strategy.

The university term didn't start until March, so Amy encouraged Lucas to find a temporary job. The more money they made as a backup, the better off they would be. They pooled the money they earned and opened a joint account for easy access. Now, either of them could pay bills and go shopping. They had settled everything by the time Lucas started his course, but all the planning in the world hadn't prepared either of them for how hard the next four years would be.

Amy trudged home after her nighttime shift. Jack, her boss, extended her hours, and now Amy worked three nights a week. Her other job kept her busy during the day, and while the money she earned kept pace with their living costs and Lucas' expenses, there was never any left. Amy longed to have a meal at a restaurant with Lucas, but their shifts rarely coincided. He was on duty tonight, but she decided they would go out on his next night off; a date night was just what she needed. There was no point in working herself to death if she didn't have some fun along the way.

The light filtered through the blinds as Amy rolled over. What had awakened her? When the door slid open, her eyes focused on her boyfriend. Lucas looked wiped out, and his eyes locked on hers as he approached the bed.

"Sorry, babe. I didn't mean to wake you. I'm so tired that my body doesn't do what I want, hence the clumsy entrance. Go back to sleep; I'm just going to shower."

"Do you want a drink or something to eat? I'm awake now so that I can get you something."

"Amy, I'm so tired my brain doesn't work. Once I've showered, I want to sleep for a long time."

"Okay."

Amy climbed out of bed and grabbed a glass of water. She was tired when she went to bed earlier, but Lucas looked worse. His skin was sallow, and his face had lines of fatigue. Lucas walked out of the bathroom with a towel around his waist as she returned from the kitchen. Amy's eyes ran over his chest, sprinkled with hair, and zeroed in on the tattoo on his bicep. Her gaze ran down his flat belly towards the hair partly covered by the towel. As her blood heated, she heard Lucas groan.

"Can it wait? I don't have the energy."

"Climb into bed, Luc. I can do the work, and you can lie there."

She grinned. "I promise to be gentle."

After navigating through the first hectic year, Amy suggested they take time out for a holiday. While Lucas doubted their ability to pay for time away, Amy was adamant. They had both been working long hours, and she wanted the time to reaffirm her connection with Lucas. There was no point in working toward their goal if they lost their bond in the pursuit. Being in the same place simultaneously would improve their 'ships in the night' relationship.

Amy asked for a week off, and with Lucas having holidays for the Christmas break, it was the perfect time to have a holiday. The decision to visit Amy's parents was an easy one because Amy had to work over the Christmas break so that they would celebrate Christmas early. The trip to Honeybrook was an easy commute once they left the traffic behind. While she and Lucas had argued about the cost of the car he believed he needed, Amy was glad that only her return trip would be on the bus. While staying at her parents' house, Lucas and Amy spent private time together, and she felt sad that time had passed so quickly. The connection she sought to strengthen had firmed, and Amy hoped it was enough to keep them focused throughout the coming year. Because Amy had to return to work, but Lucas was going to his parents to celebrate Christmas, the two parted company the night before Amy left.

Amy said on her last night with her parents, "Am I a horrible person to be jealous of Lucas spending time with his parents? He needed a holiday because the hospital and university work their students hard, but I hate that I must keep working while he has a break."

Bart Madden looked at his daughter and said, "I believe you are getting the worst of this deal. I spoke to him yesterday about his commitment, and he assured me he would keep his promise to pay for you once he qualified."

Amy nodded. "I'm sure he will do the right thing; it's just that he has nearly three months before the uni goes back, and at this time of year, it would be easy to get a casual job. Another income, no matter how temporary, would ease things a little. I haven't had new clothes or haircuts since we started this madness."

Audrey Madden looked at her daughter with concern.

"Why didn't you tell me that when you arrived? I'm sure my regular hairdresser would have fit you in, and I could have done that and bought you some clothes for your Christmas present. You shouldn't have to go without to make Lucas's life easier after he qualifies."

CHAPTER 1

Four years later

Amy returned from work to find that Lucas had been home and gone out again. She recalled the last few months and realised that she and Lucas rarely saw each other. Once, their schedules coincided, but now they were never at home together. Amy complained that all she did was work and pay his bills, and he left his dirty washing around or wrote her a brief note. Lucas gave her the same answer that he had used for four years.

"I am busy at work."

"Nobody works twenty-four-seven, as you claim. Surely you can spend the occasional afternoon or morning with me. Sometimes, you don't even come home at night. I don't want to sound needy, but I've supported you for four years. I want to see you sometimes. Can we work out your schedule and have a meal together soon?"

"You will have to be patient. Graduation is only two months away. Things will change then."

A strange look flicked in his eyes for a fleeting moment, but it disappeared so fast that Amy couldn't decide what it was.

The two months dragged by, and Lucas did not try to be home more often. Amy gritted her teeth. When he graduated, she intended to insist they take a holiday, and as soon as he started working, she would enrol in the veterinary course that was her goal. For four years, she had paid the rent, food, Lucas's books and fees, and whatever else he needed. A few weeks ago, she had to pay for his car registration and new tyres for the car. Lucas was a bottomless pit that sucked up everything she earned.

When graduation day arrived, Amy was hardly able to contain her excitement. The plan she and Lucas had hatched four long years ago was partially completed. The next part of the project was for her. She knew this day was coming up, so Amy had squirrelled away a few dollars each week and had treated herself to a haircut yesterday. She bought a new dress at the outlet shop across from the bar. She was applying makeup when Lucas walked out of the bedroom.

"Why are you dressed up? Don't you have to go to work?"

Amy gave him a disbelieving look.

"Today is your graduation day, isn't it?"

"Ah. Yeah."

"Do you think I worked my arse off doing two jobs for four years, and I'm not coming? I know you must be at the uni before me, but can't we go together? You've got a coupon for campus parking, so we won't have to walk so far."

"I thought you'd be working. I didn't get you a ticket for the ceremony."

Amy gaped at him in disbelief. "Well then, Doc, you'd better scramble to find me one. Otherwise, I will pick an empty seat, sit in it, and hope the occupants don't arrive."

Lucas ran his hands through his hair. Amy noticed the recent cut and the blond streaks for the first time.

"I'm glad my money paid for your expensive hairdo. I've been saving for months for my haircut and to buy this dress from an outlet shop. We must talk when the ceremony ends, and the celebrations finish."

After a few phone calls, Lucas found a ticket for Amy. They arrived at the uni together, and Lucas headed off to the graduates' room, and Amy found a seat a few rows back from the front. The presentation was long and tedious, but Amy had no intention of missing it. She smiled to herself; in a few years, this would be her. When they called Lucas's name, Amy's heart filled with pride. The celebration was her triumph, too. They had achieved their aim, and Lucas had a small debt to pay after he started full-time work. Now, it was her turn.

Amy filed out of her seat at the end of the presentation as others moved away. Amy moved amongst the crowd as other graduates approached family and friends, trying to find her boyfriend. Amy scanned the area, attempting to locate Lucas. He knew where she was sitting, so why hadn't he come to her? Frustration building, Amy decided that she needed a vantage point. She climbed the steps leading to the stage; now that she could see over the crowd, she saw Lucas, accompanied by a young woman, chatting to an older couple.

Once again, making her way through the crowd, Amy reached Lucas.

Amy threw her arms around him.

"Congratulations, Luc. We have completed part one of the plan." When he turned toward her, Amy realised the young woman had her hand on his arm.

"Are you going to introduce me to your friends?"

"Ah, Amy, this is Clarissa and her parents, Rod and Stella Marshall."

Amy smiled at the couple and exchanged greetings.

"I don't want to be possessive, but why is Clarissa holding onto your arm?"

Lucas's face went red, but he stood straight and looked Amy in the eye.

"Clarissa is my fiancé. We became engaged two months ago. I'm sorry, but I need a woman who understands medicine by my side."

Amy stared at Lucas for a moment. Tears welled in her eyes, and a lump formed in her throat. When her temper replaced sorrow, she said, "So while we've been living in a de facto relationship, and I've worked my arse off to pay for your medical training, you became engaged to another woman? I'm confused. Were you cheating on me, or were you cheating on her? Did I pay for that rock your fiancé is wearing? And what of my veterinary course?"

Lucas ignored the question of the valid owner of the enormous engagement ring.

"Clarissa and I intend to open a clinic, so paying for your course is out of the question."

Arm's face flushed, and she swung her hand at Lucas, slapping him. The sound of the slap reverberated around the place where they stood, and curious glances shot their way.

"You bastard. How could you do this to me? You promised me. In the beginning, when I asked you if you would revoke, you promised me you wouldn't. My Father questioned you the last time we stayed with my parents, and you told him you were a man of your word and would keep your promise."

Nausea welled in her stomach, and she wrapped her arms around herself. As the tears rolled down her cheeks, Amy turned to face the horrified couple watching the proceedings.

"Lucas and I have spent the last four years living together in a de facto relationship. We agreed on a plan. I have worked two jobs in the last four years, so Lucas qualified with minimum debts. He was going to repay the favour when he got a job. Do you want your daughter married to a man with no integrity? He's a cheater and a liar. I'm sure your daughter could do much better."

Lucas's future in-laws looked shocked by Amy's announcement, and she hoped that the parents withdrew their funds and left her cheating boyfriend high and dry.

Tears continued to fall as the enormity of Lucas's betrayal hit home.

"Give me the car keys, Luc."

"No. I need the car. We are going out to celebrate. You can catch a taxi home."

"What are you celebrating? Are you celebrating pulling off the biggest con of your life, or are you celebrating that you snagged some rich chick who will foot your bills for life? You disgust me."

Amy raised her voice. "I want the car; getting a taxi is not an option. You seem to forget I have no money, you spent it all on the fashionable hairdo and the rock on your fiance's hand. When I discover how much that ring cost, I will send you the bill unless you want me to send it to your beloved or her parents. At no time did our agreement cover engagement rings or fancy dinners for you and some woman, but considering your amnesia regarding your promise, I shouldn't be surprised. Give me the frigging keys before I start a scene that calls attention to your despicable behaviour. I can shout and make a fuss if you want."

Grudgingly, Lucas handed over the keys. Amy grabbed the keys and strode away, sobbing.

CHAPTER 2

Amy held it together on the drive home, but once inside the flat, despair hit her. She wasted four years of her life, not to mention the money she paid. Her dream of becoming a vet with very few debts was gone. Lucas left her with very little; her car and clothes were all she had now that he had moved on to someone else who could bankroll his future. Her cheating boyfriend sucked up the money she earned, and she would need to work both jobs just to put money behind her.

Amy looked around the room, and the realisation that Lucas had no discarded clothes strewn around hit her. A search in the bedroom and bathroom showed that Lucas had removed many of his belongings. How did he manage that? While she sweated and worked herself almost beyond endurance to make ends meet, the louse had been removing his belongings so that he wouldn't have to return when it became clear that he was reneging on his promise. Looking around, Amy realised she had foiled Lucas's plans by not going to work. She was sure that he intended to remove the last items while she was at work—any wonder the cad had shown surprise and annoyance at her insistence that she attend the graduation ceremony. Amy wondered if she had gone to work, would she have arrived home to find all of Lucas's belongings gone and a note for her on the kitchen bench?

After sitting for hours, stewing, Amy decided to retaliate. A search of the car turned up a receipt for the engagement ring and a note from Carissa. The price on the receipt made Amy cringe. How did Lucas fleece her for that much money without her noticing? He had unexplained expenses, but Amy was so glad to be near the end that she ignored his bills. After further investigation, Amy found Clarissa's surname and home address in Lucas' diary. Taking the leather-bound volume as insurance, Amy headed back to her apartment.

What to do to pay the cheating slimeball back? She considered her choices and decided on several things she could do. Amy called a removal company to come and pack Lucas' belongings. Even though he removed most of his clothes, his medical books and other personal things remained. She directed her next act of revenge to the car she maintained during their time together. A phone call to the motor registration board told her how to cancel Lucas's car registration.

Early the next day, Amy drove to the motor registration office and cancelled the registration on the car. After cashing in his number plates, she got trade plates to move the vehicle to a tyre depot. A refund on the new tyres Amy paid for two weeks ago would fund her living expenses while sorting out her finances. Amy's appeal surprised the tyre retailers, but they removed the wheels from the car without fuss. After a consultation, the two parties agreed on the price of the tyres and wheels. Amy booked a tilt truck to pick up the disabled vehicle and deliver it to Clarissa's house. Once the removalist dumped Lucas's possessions on Clarissa's driveway, Amy's revenge would almost be complete. She was unsure what to do about the engagement ring; should she call the police and report it stolen? The only thing that stopped her was that maybe the woman, Clarissa, didn't know about Lucas's living arrangements.

After changing the locks on the flat doors, Amy vacuumed and washed until the place was spotless. She wanted the bond back, and as Lucas paid half of the money, she thought it fair that she should receive the entire sum. Once Amy returned the keys and old locks and keys, there was nothing left to do. She emailed her resignation to her bosses and left Mountfield without a backward glance.

Amy wended through the afternoon traffic, her radio blaring the latest pop songs. The upbeat music did nothing to raise her spirits, but she decided to pretend everything was okay until it was. But her immediate concern was how to tell her parents that after four years of working day and night, she was broke, with no immediate job prospects.

Once Amy left the city streets, the open highway stretched ahead. In retrospect, some signs should have alerted her to Lucas's lack of commitment to their plan; endless nights spent alone was a red flag, but Amy trusted that the man she had supported for four years would come through for her. What a fool she was! No one worked twenty-four seven and didn't make it home to their bed for days on end, but in her defence, she was so tired with the endless routine of work and more work that she didn't have the energy to push the issue.

When she gave her relationship with Lucas any thought, she knew the spark between them had died, beaten down by endless work hours and time spent apart. Amy knew her relationship with Lucas was past being salvaged, but it never occurred to her that he would double-cross her in such a ruthless and unfeeling manner. She had wasted four years and a lot of money to support the bastard and had nothing to show for her hard work.

After a short stop at a petrol station to refuel and visit the facilities, Amy started on the last leg of her trip. When her navigation became automatic, Amy knew she was minutes from home. Amy had made sure to visit occasionally during her time away, but the time between visits increased with her packed work schedule. Now, she had to tell her parents that her years of neglect and extended absences were all in vain.

Amy arrived home as night approached. Seeing her would surprise her parents, and the explanations might stretch into the night. When the front light flicked on, Amy knew that her time for deliberating was over. Her Mother's startled exclamation brought her Father to the front door. Both parents rushed to hug her. The well of tears that Amy banked up during the drive burst, and she sobbed In her Mother's arms. Her Father took charge, sheepherding both women inside as he unloaded Amy's things.

The kitchen warmth wrapped around her like a security blanket, and Amy sank into a chair.

"Sorry, mum. I've driven without crying, but I'm so sad and angry that I couldn't hold on anymore."

Amy's mum gave her a quick hug.

"Let's get the kettle on, and when your dad finishes putting your bags in your room, you can share your troubles with us. Your unannounced arrival is a surprise. Today is the first time you have visited without Lucas."

Amy hiccoughed a sob. "Well, you will need to get used to his absence. I have finished with the lying, cheating piece of shit."

When Amy's Father settled into a set near his daughter, he said, "Do you want to tell us what happened that made you flee Mountfield?"

As Amy recounted what had happened, neither of her parents spoke. Amy could tell that he was furious by the flush on her dad's face, and her mom's tears warmed Amy's heart. Her parents loved her, and both would support her with whatever she did. But now, she wanted to bask in her parent's love.

"I want to tear the mongrel limb from limb. How could that scum walk away with a clear conscience when Lucas has reneged on your agreement? I guess you got nothing in writing?"

"No. But I had a win, though."

Her Father chuckled when Amy described her actions regarding the car and Lucas' belongings.

"What do they say about a woman scorned? It's nice to see you retaliate. If the other woman is sensible, she will drop him. And with the flat locked up and on the market for lease, it will force him to pay the rent or go elsewhere."

After a moment, Amy's mum said, "What do you have in mind for the future?"

"In the immediate future, I hope to eat and intend to sleep for a long time. After that, I will decide on my future. Becoming a veterinarian with very few debts isn't in my future. I'm glad I had enough petrol to fill my car; otherwise, I might have had to hitchhike home. I considered reporting the ring stolen because it cost a packet, but I decided that maybe the woman didn't know he was a cheater. I hate to think he will have more money if she calls it quits and he pawns the ring. Do you realise I'm broke? He took every penny I earned and then lied and cheated."

CHAPTER 3

Amy spent the next six months recuperating from her ordeal. The dole was great, and the government handout helped her with her daily expenses. After the fiasco with Lucas, Amy found it hard to motivate herself. What did she have to look forward to? The waves of fatigue rolled over her, and her wan visage no longer shocked Amy when she looked in the mirror. Simply getting out of bed some days was an overwhelming task that she couldn't complete, and really, what was the point? It was easier to roll over and pretend the day hadn't started.

Ruth Benson, Amy's Mother, walked out onto the veranda and sat next to Amy as she sat staring into space. The change in Amy distressed her; to see her formerly vivacious, happy daughter try to drag herself through the day broke her heart. Gosh, if she could get her hands on Lucas, she would wring his neck. Ruth was not usually a vindictive woman, but she hoped Lucas's medical clinic fell in a heap, assuming the fiance's parents hadn't stopped the relationship. Ruth patted her daughter's arm and drew in a deep breath.

"Amy, you can't spend your life mourning the years and money you lost. Nothing will give you back the time you wasted and will not fill your bank account. I hate to see you so listless and unmotivated. You need to reclaim your life. Don't let what Lucas did define you. He has to live knowing that he cheated you, and Karma will catch up with him. But you, my darling, need to move forward."

"I know I have to do something, but I'm always tired."

The dark circles under her eyes and the grey tinge to her face confirmed Amy's complaint. Amy had lost weight, and her clothes hung in a way that concerned Ruth.

"Right, that does it! I will call Doctor Christa and book an appointment for you. I will tell her it's for a full check-up, and I will go with you so that you can tell her everything."

"Okay. I'm sick of myself. If the doctor can help, that would be a good move."

Ruth Benson sighed with relief and disappeared to make the phone call.

Amy's visit to the doctor proved worthwhile. Dr Christa was nothing if not thorough, taking blood tests and monitoring Amy's pulse and blood pressure. She sympathised with Amy, shocked that a man supposed to be compassionate could treat a friend in such a poor way. After Dr Christa diagnosed iron deficiency and depression, Amy left the doctor's surgery with prescriptions. The iron supplement was to help boost Amy's iron levels until she stabilised her eating habits, but the antidepressants were a long-term medication. The doctor wanted Amy to raise her physical exercise level because being active was a good way of fighting depression.

Amy walked each day, sometimes with her Mother and other times alone. She considered getting a dog to accompany her on her walks. Still, after considerable thought, Amy rejected the idea. Who knew where she would eventually move to? Many rental properties refused to have pets on their premises. One Saturday morning, Amy encountered many people walking, running and jogging. While they moved at their own pace, the crowd seemed to be together. When her curiosity got the better of her, Amy joined a group of ladies walking smartly along. The women were happy to share their information about an activity called Parkrun. Parkrun was an exercise group where the participants walked, jogged, or ran five kilometres. Could she do that? With nothing to lose, Amy turned up at the venue at six forty-five on Saturday morning dressed for exercise. Her fear of being embarrassed at her lack of ability disappeared when she saw the mix of people, from young kids to elderly participants, preparing to exercise. The officials welcomed her, and for the first time, her exercise wasn't a chore. People encouraged others, and the runners returning from the halfway mark high-fived people coming towards them. Amy realised that despite Lucas's shabby treatment, other people encouraged and supported the folks around them. With this knowledge, Amy knew she could move forward.

As she became more active, Amy's demeanour changed. The dark circles under her eyes disappeared, and at mealtimes, she ate. Now, Amy had to decide on her future. With its expenses, the university was further away than before she agreed with Lucas. After checking the job sites for employment opportunities, Amy decided on an administrative business certificate at the local TAFE. Many online and print ads asked for business administrators and personal assistants, so her study area seemed a good choice. Her unemployment gave her a discount, and the course became affordable. The class was only twelve months, and the participant gained the skills to work in an office. Amy could do most of the course online, which postponed the need to move away from her family's support. If she ever managed to enrol in a veterinary course, her business qualifications would help her run her own company.

Thoughts of her dream job always made Amy sad, so she decided to push ahead and put her desire to take a veterinary course aside. The only way to get her dream job without crippling debt was to work for a year or two and save every penny she made.

CHAPTER 4

Amy surveyed the place that was to be home for the near future. The furnished house provided what she needed, and Amy was only required to bring her clothes and toiletries to her new home. Because of her financial problems, Amy opted for a house-sitting job instead of looking for a place. The owners of this lovely place were touring Europe for six months, so Amy had free accommodation until the trip ended. By then, she should have saved enough to find her apartment, but this house-sitting was a great way to get free accommodation so she might do that again. The cost of electricity and gas was a cheap way to pay for a home.

After completing her administrative business certificate, Amy applied for an assistant to the PA at Maddox Incorporated. She had no idea what the company did, but she supposed it didn't matter as an office assistant. Dressed in a business suit, Amy parked her car on a side street and walked to the business.

The foyer of the building was large and manned by a guard at the front desk. The security man smiled at Amy.

"Good morning. Can I help you, Miss?"

"Good morning to you, too. I am here for an interview with Mr Robert James. My name is Amy Benson."

The man checked the clipboard he held in his hand.

"Ah, here you are. Mr James is expecting you. Please take the lift to the second door. The receptionist there will help you."

With a cherry wave, Amy moved towards the lift.

Once the lift deposited Amy on the second floor, she walked towards the desk in the middle of the room. A smiling face greeted her.

"Good morning. You must be Amy Benson; Kent called to tell me you were going upstairs. I have a questionnaire that Mr James has prepared for you, and after you complete the form, I will show you through to his office."

The questionnaire asked the usual questions, and when Amy handed the sheet back to the receptionist, she rose to escort Amy to the human resources officer's office. Mr James rose as Amy entered the office and extended his hand for a handshake. Amy had to resist the urge to wipe her hand on her pants leg after the handshake. Although Amy couldn't pinpoint what made her squirm, there was something off about the HR man. His gaze lingered on her breasts, and his pleasant manner looked forced.

"Well, my dear, what do you know about the company." Amy cringed at the form of his address but pushed it aside. After Lucas's betrayal, she needed this job to fill the coffers and her self-esteem. What did it matter if the HR man had no understanding of sexual harassment? His focus never met her eyes as she filled him on the little she knew. With his gaze fixed on her breasts, Mr James took no notes and asked no other questions. After a moment of silence, the man got control of himself and stood.

"I think you are qualified for the job, but Mrs Yardley is overwhelmed with work and will accept any help she can get. Follow me, and I will introduce you to her."

After his scrutiny of her breasts, Amy was glad that the man didn't suggest she go first. The thought of him ogling her bottom made her stomach cringe. Mrs Yardley was a plump lady who appeared to be in her late forties or early fifties. When Amy met her, she understood the term 'mutton dressed up as lamb.' With a determined smile, Amy offered her hand to the woman who would supervise her work here in the office.

"I'll leave you in Mrs Yardley's capable hands. But call me if you need any extra help." As the man left, Amy vowed never to call the man.

Amy watched Mr James leave the room. She was now in Mrs Yardley's hands, but the woman didn't look impressed by her presence.

"What qualifications do you have besides being young and attractive?"

Amy gasped at the woman's offensive question. She lifted her chin; she glared at the woman.

"I have a certificate in business administration, and Mr James felt that I was qualified as I was to be your assistant. Regarding your comment on my appearance, I was unaware that one qualification was surliness and unattractiveness. I will let Mr James know that you find me wanting. Good day to you."

Amy stalked along the corridor to Robert James's office. She admitted that she was desperate for a job, but this place gave off weird vibes, and the offensive Mrs Yardley firmed her opinion of the business. After the number of put-downs Lucas had thrown at her, Amy would not accept that treatment again.

When Amy knocked on the human resources manager's office, a man called for her to enter. Mr James had a flushed face and a line of sweat upon his upper lip.

"What can I do for you, Miss Benson?"

"I came in to tell you that Mrs Yardley does not think my qualifications are good enough and doesn't like that I am a young female. I would never have applied for the job if I had known what a weird set-up this was. Good luck finding a more qualified applicant than I, and make sure the applicant is male or an ugly, fat female."

Amy stormed out of the office and heard Mr James berating Mrs Yardley. Once she arrived in the foyer, the doorman, Kent, smiled at her.

"How did it go, Miss Benson?"

"I'm too good looking for the job. Mrs Yardley wants a male assistant or a fat, ugly woman."

Kent looked shocked at this announcement.

"It's okay; that place has a weird vibe. I'll apply to other places I considered."

"Wait, Miss Benson. I'm unsure of the strange feeling you got in there, but the CEO is nice. I can't imagine him approving of Mrs Yardley's requirements. Give me a minute; even if you don't want a job here anymore, you deserve an apology for how the staff treated you."

Kent picked up the phone and punched in numbers. He pressed the speaker button, and a deep male voice answered.

"Kent, is there a problem?"

"There is no security problem, but you have a staffing problem."

Amy heard a chuckle, and then the voice said, "When did my staffing become your business, my friend."

"Since today. A qualified young lady, Miss Benson, applied for the assistant job with Mrs Yardley. Mr James gave her the job, but Mrs Yardley threw her out because she didn't think her qualifications were good enough and she was too young and attractive."

A deep sigh was the response to Kent's comment.

"Am I on speaker, Kent?"

"Yes, sir."

"Miss Benson, you have my most sincere apologies. If Mr James believes you are right for the job, then the job is yours if you wish. I will deal with Mrs Yardley now, and there will be no more harassment. If she continues to bully you, I will fire her, and you can have her job."

"Thank you, sir, for the apology. I'm not sure I want the job, though."

"Why don't you go to the café across the road for morning tea? Whatever you decide, please come back and let us know. I will haul Mrs Yardley into line, and she will behave herself if she wants her job."

The speaker beeped.

"Mrs Yardley, will you please come into the office?"

Once Mrs Yardley sat, the CEO, Dean Turner, swivelled his chair to face her.

"I am waiting for Mr James to join us."

While waiting for his HR manager, Dean fiddled with the computer before him. The knock on the door announced Robert James's arrival, and Dean Turner pointed the chair to his left. He focused on his male counterpart after giving the computer his attention for a few moments longer.

"Robert, please give me a rundown on Miss Benson."

"The young lady has a certificate in office administration, but she has limited experience to back up the qualification. If the job were your PA, I might hesitate to hire her because of her lack of practice, but as an assistant to Mrs Yardley, I felt she could handle the job well. At her interview, she presented herself well and was open and friendly. This job is not challenging, and I don't believe we will get a more qualified person applying."

Dean nodded his head as he listened to his HR manager. He looked over at Mrs Yardley, and the smirk on her face gave him cause for concern. What was wrong with the woman?

"Okay, that sounds workable. What are your concerns, Mrs Yardley, about the applicant?"

"A pretty face swayed Mr James. The girl has no experience in a fast-paced work environment, and a piece of paper saying she's qualified doesn't mean she can do the job. I don't want a female who gets by on her looks and not her ability."

"What you're saying is that she hasn't had enough experience. How do we prove she's qualified unless we believe her credentials and try her? Robert, were there any references?"

"Yes. Miss Benson had references from the company where she did her work experience. Both letters were glowing endorsements; one from the CEO and one from her supervisor."

"Hm. Let us give Miss Benson a try. We'll hire her on a two-month probationary period, and at the end of that time, we will review her performance. Mrs Yardley, I will have no bullying or harassment of the new hire. If you need an assistant, then we have found one. Don't mess this up because I will not hire a replacement if she leaves because of you. Are we clear on that?"

Mrs Yardley's surly agreement put Dean on edge. If the girl still wanted the job, would he need to keep his eye on what was happening in the next room?

CHAPTER 5

Before agreeing to the job, Amy did a Google search on both the company and the CEO. She was interested in finding out what kind of man ran a company where harassment and hostility levels were so high. The company had only one hit, but Dean Turner had three hits. The first site showed a very handsome couple. The man was as good-looking as the woman on his arm. Included in the article were information on the company and the personal details of Dean and his fiancé. Her breath caught in her throat when she clicked on the other location. The headline of the newspaper showed the mangled wreck of a car. The story detailed the horrific accident that injured Dean and his fiancé, Margot. Margot was the vehicle's driver, and she escaped with minor injuries. In the passenger seat, when the utility T-boned their car, Dean suffered severe injuries. He suffered a broken leg and hip, broken ribs, a fractured arm and facial injuries. The breaks had healed, but the damage to his face had left him with permanent scars.

While her boss's information was enlightening, Amy wasn't sure how long she could work with his weird management team. Working on the theory that beggars can't be choosey, Amy took the job for the time being. But she intended to keep her eye on the job vacancies as a safeguard. Amy's main task was to update her boss's calendar, respond to email inquiries, and type reports. The work went well for the first few days, and although she didn't like the woman she worked with, Amy kept the end goal in sight. She would do this job while looking around for other choices.

Mrs Yardley was passively aggressive, and Amy didn't know what she had done to the woman to make her dislike her so much. The first conversation between the two women happened during the first hour of Amy's employment.

"Are you driving to work?" Mrs Yardley asked.

"Yes, I have no public transport, so I drive."

"Well, I hope you don't think you can park in the company car park. That is only for upper management and long-term employees; park in the street."

"Mrs Yardley, it will please you to know that a peasant like me understands the business hierarchy. I will continue to park in the street," Amy said.

Amy gritted her teeth and kept working. No one should have to put up with uncomfortable work conditions. The woman was impossible, and the search for a new job would be on in earnest now.

Little by little, the workload on Amy's desk increased. Every time Amy looked at the woman, Mrs Yardley focused on the computer, her fingers tapping across the keyboard. If the PA continuously worked, as she seemed to, from where was the extra work originating?

Amy gave herself a brief break and headed towards the ladies' toilets. When she attempted to enter, the door handle didn't budge. It appeared the bathrooms were locked. While she stood still, trying to decide what to do, one of the other women came past her.

"Hi, my name is Natalie. Don't bother trying the door handle. That sicko James locks the lady's toilets, so we have to ask him for the key. He gives you a five-minute lecture on wasting the company time if you ask him for the key. Most of us try to hang on and use the restroom downstairs. During our monthlies, we sometimes have to use the toilets up here; it is humiliating to have him questioning our toilet habits."

Amy pursed her lips. "That is appalling. Are the men's toilets locked?"

Natalie shook her head. "No, according to Mr James, men don't waste the company's time when they go to the bathroom."

"God, this place gets weirder and weirder."

Amy rubbed her temples; the pain that lingered all day had become a full-blown headache. It was six o'clock, and Amy had just finished the work that Mrs Yardley dumped on her desk when the woman left at four o'clock. Amy's stomach grumbled, reminding her she hadn't eaten since morning tea. After closing the computer, Amy realised the journey home would be uncomfortable without a toilet stop. There was no point in checking the ladies' bathrooms. For a moment, Amy considered using the men's toilets but remembered Mr James walking along the corridor, checking that he had locked everything, including the men's toilets.

The building was dark; hers was the only light visible. What would stop Amy from using the CEO's toilet if no one was around? The journey home would be far more comfortable than driving forty minutes with a full bladder. Mr Turner's door was unlocked, as Amy discovered when she turned the handle. She eased the door open and glanced around the dim room. As Amy crept along, she ran her hand over the wall, trying to locate a light switch. When her hand brushed the button, she flicked it, and the room lit up. Before she could take another step, a voice bellowed, "Turn off the damn light."

Amy jumped, the shock rendering her speechless. She scrambled to find the elusive switch and kill the lights in the room. When she looked around, searching for the angry man, she discovered him hunched over the computer. A USB plugged into the laptop lit up the keyboard, so the man sat in almost total darkness.

"Who the hell are you, and what are you doing sneaking into my office?"

"Um, I'm Amy, and I need to use the toilet."

"May I ask why the ladies' toilets aren't good enough for you?"

"Please, Mr Turner, can we have this discussion in a minute? I need the facilities, and if I wait much longer, there will be a puddle on the floor."

"For god's sake, go, but we haven't finished this conversation."

The words had only just left Dean Turner's mouth when he heard the door of the bathroom slam shut. Who was the woman, and why was she in his office after six o'clock? The intrusion had shattered his concentration, and as soon as the woman emerged from the bathroom, he intended to sort out this absurd situation.

Amy splashed water on her face and finger-combed her hair. She needed to devise an explanation that didn't sound like she was complaining. Nothing made the boss angrier than endless complaints from the workers. She shrugged her shoulders, and with her chin tilted up, Amy walked out of the bathroom. As she approached the desk, Mr Turner held up his hand.

"That's close enough."

Amy stood halfway between his desk and the door. She realised he sat sideways, so she could only see his profile. It felt weird talking to the side of his face.

"I am sorry for intruding. I was ready to go home but needed to use the bathroom before leaving."

"Why were you heading home? For God's sake, woman, it's six-thirty. What time are you supposed to leave?"

"My finishing time is five o'clock, but I had too much work to leave then."

"How could you have too much work? You're the assistant, damn it. What is Mrs Yardley doing? Why isn't she here helping if this work is vital?"

After the barrage of questions, Amy shrugged her shoulders. "I swore to myself that I wouldn't tell you what is going on because I don't want you to label me as a whinger or a troublemaker. At four o'clock, Mrs Yardley loads my desk with paperwork from her table and goes home. Before she leaves, she stresses that I must finish the work before I leave."

"So, my PA goes early and leaves you with her incomplete tasks?"

"Yes."

"Does she say why she is leaving at four?"

"No, she does not."

Amy watched as confusion spread across Dean Turner's face. Maybe telling him what was happening might make him check his workforce more often.

"Okay, I'll fix that. But that doesn't explain why you need to use my bathroom. What's wrong with the ladies' toilets?"

"Mr James locks the ladies' toilets during the day."

Dean spun around to look at Amy, forgetting to shield his face. "Don't be ridiculous. Why would James lock the ladies' bathroom during the day?"

"Because, according to Mr James, women waste the company's time congregating in the bathroom. Most of the ladies here hang on and use the toilets downstairs. If you need to go to the toilet and ask him for the key, Mr James gives you a five-minute speech on employees' responsibilities. It's so humiliating."

"Good grief! That's a sexual harassment claim waiting to happen. What could the man be thinking? I will fix that first thing in the morning. Is there something else I should know?"

"No, I don't think so."

Dean stood, and Amy realised how tall he was. He styled his sandy hair, and his suit looked tailor-made. The man filled out the suit well, thought Amy. Her boss walked through the dim reception room as she collected her bag.

"It's raining; I have an umbrella to walk you to the car."

His offer took Amy aback, but she was happy to have an escort to her car. When they exited the building, Dean turned right, and Amy stopped.

"Ah, my car is this way, Mr Turner."

"The car park is here under the building. Why are you parked on the street?"

"Mrs Yardley told me the car park was only for senior staff and long-term employees. She was at pains to point out that I am on a two-month trial for the moment, so I had to park in the street."

"Good grief! Have I employed stupid people here? Come with me, and I will drive you around to your car. Walking the streets at this time of night is dangerous."

Amy followed her boss to the underground car park, grateful she didn't have to walk along the wet, dark street to her car. The night before, silence and the sound of her footsteps on the empty road had given her the creeps. A flash of lights and a chirping sound emanated from the lone car still parked in the lot; this flash vehicle belonged to her boss. After following her directions, her boss pulled alongside the small coupe that was Amy's transport.

She noticed that the overhead light was off as she opened the door. Despite her having seen Dean's face in the office when he forgot himself and faced her, he was self-conscious about his scarred face.

"Thanks very much, boss."

"Call me Dean and repay the debt by parking in the staff car park tomorrow." He gave her a wave and drove away.

CHAPTER 6

The following day, Amy arrived before Mrs Yardley, and with no immediate tasks to complete, she detoured to the lunchroom. A high-end coffee machine sat on the bench, and as Amy was desperate for a drink, she filled the machine and poured the coffee beans into the dispenser at the top of the device. The aroma of freshly brewed coffee wafted through the room, making her even more anxious about the drink. When the liquid began to drip from the spout, Amy placed a cup underneath and went to find some milk. The fridge was bare, so she set to searching the cupboards. Surely, there would be long-life milk somewhere here if there was no fresh milk.

"What the dickens are you doing?"

Amy jumped, startled by the angry voice. Turning to face Mrs Yardley, Amy shrugged.

"I am setting up the coffee machine."

"Who permitted you to set up the machine.? The coffee is not for the likes of you; it is for senior staff and management. And while I am thinking about your transgressions, is that your red Corolla in the car park? I told you that you have to park in the street."

"Mrs Yardley, you are a horrid, lying cow. Last night at six-thirty, when I finished the work you dumped on my desk as you left, Mr Turner walked me to my car and was outraged at the thought that I had walked to my car in the dark the previous night. He told me to park in the car park because it is for all staff. So if you have a problem with that, I suggest you talk to Mr Turner. And knowing your record with honesty, I doubt your take on who is allowed to use the coffee machine."

Amy turned, ignoring the woman, and poured herself a cup of coffee. Once she had doctored it to her taste, she walked from the room and left the other woman gaping.

Amy discovered later in the day that provoking the other woman backfired. Mrs Yardley smirked at Amy as she walked out at four oçlock, having loaded Amy's desk with folders. Amy sighed at the pile of work on her desk; it would take hours to get through the folders the other woman had thrown on her desk. Amy worked until five o'clock, collected the unfinished folders and placed them on Mrs Yardley's desk. The horrid woman could start the day with her pile of folders. Before walking out, Amy noted the file numbers, anxious to see if Mrs Yardley was leaving her with folders that she should finish and if the rapid typing the woman did was assigned work, online shopping, or games.

After bidding Kent a good night, Amy investigated the food outlets near the business. Cooking for one person was tedious, and although she generally made enough to freeze, sometimes she required variety. When Amy walked into a small restaurant serving Italian food, the aroma of the cooked food made her stomach grumble, and she opted to eat in. The server walked her towards a table, and as she passed a man seated in the corner, Amy realised that the man was Dean Turner. What should she do? Did she ignore him or acknowledge him? Amy realised he sat in such a way that the servers would only see the undamaged side of his face, but if she stood to the side, she could greet him without making him feel uncomfortable.

"Mr Turner, this place seems to be a magnet for hungry workers."

Dean turned his head slightly. "Good evening, Miss Benson; seeing you finished your work on time is nice."

"Ah, well, all the work Mrs Yardley dumped on my desk at four o'clock when she left is mostly incomplete. I hope there was nothing urgent in the pile of folders, but I would have had to work until eight o'clock to finish the folders."

Without thinking, Dean swung his face towards Amy, and he frowned. "You said that the other night, but I thought it might have been a once-in-a-while happening, but it seems it is not. I will check with the woman in the morning to find out what she is doing. Her decision to leave early is annoying, but if she cannot complete her work and leaves it for you, that is not on."

The server delivered Dean's order, and Amy took the menu from the man and walked to the next booth.

"Ah, Miss Benson, as we are both alone, would you like to join me? If you sit at the end of the table, you won't have to see my face."

As her boss suggested, Amy moved to the end of the bench and said, "I have caught glimpses of your face, and it's a pity people make you feel like you should hide."

Dean shrugged. "It's easier this way. Mothers rush their children past me, appearing to believe my disfigurement is contagious. But enough of me, tell me about you. What do your family do? Are they close by?"

As Amy told Dean about her family and explained that an unforeseen problem had made her change her job choices, he listened attentively. She explained about house sitting and the benefits of saving rent and helping people go on extended holidays without fearing for the homes they left behind. Amy asked questions about Maddox Incorporated and how it began. Dean was an intelligent dinner companion, and when they finished their meal, he picked up the tab for her meal and his. Despite Amy's objections, Dean paid the bill and said, "You should walk out by yourself because if you walk with me, people will stare at you."

Amy shook her head. "If it makes you happy, I will, but thank you for your company tonight."

Amy walked away without looking back, but her heart ached for this intelligent, kind man who people judged by his appearance and not his character.

The following day, Mrs Yardley exited Dean's office with a scowl.

"I said you were too young and attractive for this role, and it seems the boss has taken a shine to you. If you did your work during the day, you might have been able to finish it in a good time. I have had appointments over the last week, and that's why I had to leave early, but now my health will suffer because I won't be able to attend my appointments."

"Mrs Yardley, if you have legitimate medical appointments, book them with HR and take the time off. However, I doubt your sob story because you spend all day tapping away at your keyboard but never get any work completed. You dump your incomplete work on my desk when you swan out with a sly smile at four o'clock. I am supposed to be the assistant, not the PA. We should swap titles and paychecks if you can't do your job."

The glare the woman levelled at her made Amy determined to search for job vacancies when she returned home that night.

When Mrs Yardley's intercom buzzed, the woman answered with none of the anger she had shown Amy. Amy ignored the woman as she spoke to her boss, and when the woman rose from her seat, Amy looked up. The grimace on the woman's face made her ask,

"Is there something wrong?"

"Not if you don't mind looking at a monster. That man should wear a mask so we don't have to look at him."

"Gosh, that's harsh. You can't blame Mr Turner for what happened to him, and I admire him for running a business that he started."

Mrs Yardley snorted. "Admire away all you like. You might think differently if you had to look at him."

Amy knew she was in a no-win situation and shook her head before focusing on her computer screen.

Over the next few days, Dean called the senior staff to his office, and as they entered, everyone grimaced. The lack of empathy and the level of disgust his staff expressed was horrifying, and later in the day, when Dean buzzed Mrs Yardley to make him some coffee, Amy offered to do the job instead of the woman who was already grimacing.

"Trying to win Brownie points, are you?"

"No. Seeing you find contact with Mr Turner so distasteful, I thought I would save you the job. But don't worry, you can fix the boss's coffee and take it to him."

Mrs Yardley stalked from the office toward the kitchen. When she returned, she placed the mug of coffee on Amy's desk and said, "Take that to Mr Turner."

Amy nodded and tapped on the door before she entered. Dean was sitting at his desk, raising an eyebrow, when he saw his coffee delivery girl. Despite his attempt to shield his face, Amy could see red, angry skin and wondered if it always hurt.

"Miss Benson, how did you get the job of delivering my coffee?

"Ah, Mrs Yardley asked me to deliver the drink."

There was no humour in the laugh that exploded from him.

"You mean Mrs Yardley didn't want to face me again."

Amy blushed. "Ah... I'm not sure."

CHAPTER 7

Despite Dean giving Mrs Yardley a dressing down, the woman began to load up Amy and disappear for long lunches. She left at a quarter to twelve and didn't return until one thirty. Amy was supposed to go to lunch at one but had to wait for her superior to return. Day after day, Amy waited for the woman to return before she could leave. One day, Kent commented on Amy's late lunch, and she shrugged.

"I'm reluctant to tell Mr Turner because he had to sort out the division of work when I first started, and I don't want him to think I'm a troublemaker."

"You, Miss Benson, are too kind. Would you like me to talk to Mr Turner about what the Yardley woman is doing?"

"No, I'll give it a week and speak to him if she is still doing it."

When Amy returned after lunch, Mrs Yardley smirked at her.

"Mr Turner wants to speak to you."

Amy looked mildly surprised but headed towards the office and knocked on the door. Once she entered the office, the scowling face of her boss greeted her.

"Where the hell have you been?"

Amy frowned. "Ah, I went to lunch."

"Correct me if I am wrong, but your lunch starts at one o'clock. What do you think you are doing arriving back at two o'clock? Even if you cannot add up, the clock should tell you that forty-five minutes gives you from one to quarter to two for lunch. Mrs Yardley has reported that you have taken to having long lunches for the last few weeks, which is why she has difficulty completing her work."

Dean watched the stunned expression on Amy's face, and her refusal to comment sealed her fate. He liked the girl and believed she was doing a good job, but he would fire her under the circumstances.

"Amy, you were employed on a two-month probation period so that I can fire you without notice. Collect your belongings, and I will ask security to see you out."

Dean turned away but swung around when Amy began to laugh. As the tears ran down her face, his eyes widened, and he wondered if he had triggered some mental health issues.

Amy said, "Before you call security and have them evict me, ring Kent on the front desk and ask him to come up."

"Why would I do that?"

"Because, Mr Turner, if you don't, I will sue you for wrongful dismissal and take you to the cleaners for your trouble."

Dean punched some numbers into his phone and said, "Can you come to my office."

Amy and Dean sat in silence as they waited for Kent to arrive. When he walked into the room, it surprised him to see Amy, and he smiled at her.

"What can I do for you?"

"I am about to fire Miss Benson; for some unknown reason, she has asked for you."

Kent looked at Amy and returned his observation to Dean before saying, "Why are you firing her?"

"Mrs Yardley told me that Miss Benson has habitually had an extended lunch hour over the last two weeks. She is supposed to leave at one and return at one forty-five, but she has been returning at two fifteen."

"Ah, did she now. Why don't you call the woman in? I'd be interested to hear what she has to say."

"Why do you want to hear what she has to say? We seem to have a clear breach of Miss Benson's work agreement, and I am entitled to fire her."

"Mr Turner, I am interested in hearing what the woman says because she is lying."

Dean punched the button on his intercom, and minutes after, Mrs Yardley entered, a smirk on her face. When she saw Kent, the smile faded, and she said, "Why on earth would we need the doorman to be here when you give this trollop her marching orders."

Before Dean could speak, Kent said, "Mrs Yardley, do you know what I do all day?"

The woman scowled at him. "How would I know? I suppose you open doors for people and direct them to the right elevator. What does it matter?"

"I do one other thing, Mrs Yardley. I log the movement of people into and out of the foyer. This logging means I can go downstairs and collect my log book to prove you are the one taking long lunches."

Kent turned towards Dean. "Mr Turner, Amy and I spoke about this very fact only a few days ago, but Amy didn't want you to think she was a troublesome employee. I offered to speak with you, but she left it for a few days to see if the situation improved."

Dean ran his hands through his hair. "Hell, what a mess. Mrs Yardley, why would you make up stories about Miss Benson that we can easily disprove?"

"I told you at the beginning that her face and figure were the reason she got the job, and despite her shoddy work, she still has a job."

"Okay, bring me proof of Miss Benson's shoddy work."

Mrs Yardley flushed. "Well, there is no proof because I spent all day rectifying her mistakes."

"Is that true, Miss Benson?"

"No, it is not. Mrs Yardley never checks my work."

Kent stood. "Mr Turner, do you need me any longer?"

"No, no, thanks, Kent for your input."

The office remained silent as the three occupants sat, waiting for a solution to the problem. Eventually, Amy said, "Mr Turner, pay me out, and I will leave. Working in this toxic environment is not good for my health. When you hire another person to assist Mrs Yardley, make it a fat, ugly woman or a man. Please call security to escort me out; I hope you will write me a reference to help me find other employment after this awful job."

Dean stood. "No. No to the security, no to the reference and no to your resignation. Mrs Yardley, I spoke to you when Miss Benson first began working here, and now I am talking to you again about wrongful accusations. The third time I have to settle a skirmish between you two, one that you have started, I will fire you and give Miss Benson your job. Do I make myself clear?"

Mrs Yardley glared at Amy and, refocusing on Dean, said, "Certainly, Mr Turner."

The woman stormed out of the office, and Amy sighed.

"Truly, it would be easier to let me go. Working with the woman has been trying, and now that you have given her a second warning, it will only get worse."

"Miss Benson, I run this company, not Mrs Yardley. I employ you, and if that woman thinks I will overlook her behaviour, she is mistaken. Now, return to your desk and continue your tasks, and no more talking about quitting."

Amy's concern that her work environment would deteriorate came true, and while she tried to keep her head down and complete her work promptly, the atmosphere was frosty. Mrs Yardley constantly interrupted Amy to run useless tasks, and every time Dean wanted something, the woman made Amy the messenger. Amy left on time when the workday finished, relieved to escape the toxic environment. Her job search had turned up nothing suitable in the area, and while moving would solve her problem, she had signed a six-month contract with the house owners. There were jobs in other places that would suit her, and she vowed that as soon as the homeowners returned, she would give her notice and quit.

CHAPTER 8

Amy looked at her payslip and frowned. Her pay slip showed her hours, but a separate payment was labelled *endurance.* What the hell was that payment for?

Although she and her immediate boss were not on speaking terms, Amy said,

"Mrs Yardley, what is the payment titled endurance? What does that mean?"

The woman scoffed at her. "I'm not sure you deserve the payment, but Mr Turner compensates everyone who has to face his face for the distress it causes us."

Amy frowned. "He pays you because you have face-to-face interaction with him?"

"Yes, it's a nice perk."

"A nice perk? What is wrong with you people? I have never heard anything so sick in my whole life."

Pushing her chair away, Amy stormed towards Dean's office. Without knocking on the door, she entered the room, and her boss looked up, a startled expression crossing his face. Amy's entry was so swift that Dean didn't have time to shield his face.

"What the hell are you doing?"

"How dare you include me into the pool of heartless, fickle people you employ who need extra pay because they have to look at your face. I am insulted, and I don't want the damn money for *endurance.* What kind of workplace is this when the employees must have compensation for looking at their boss?"

She saw Dean Turner's anger for the first time since she came to work for Maddox Incorporation. He stood behind his desk and glared at her.

"The kind where the boss is so severely scared that it disgusts people who have face-to-face contact with him."

Amy looked her boss in the face.

"Mr Turner, Dean, I am looking you in the face and have no desire to run out the door or find a receptacle to vomit into. The people in your employ are bloodsuckers, and you should tell them there will be no endurance money, and if they leave, hire a better calibre of people."

Dean Turner stormed around his desk to stand almost nose-to-nose with Amy.

"Look at me, Miss Benson; tell me you aren't disgusted with how I look."

Amy looked at the tight, shiny, red skin that covered Dean's cheeks. She guessed the damaged skin was from a botched plastic surgery operation, and she felt empathy and sadness that this man who was so handsome before the accident should be ashamed of how he looked now. Amy lifted her hand to touch Dean's damaged cheek. "I feel sad that you should have to hide yourself away because of something that I guess is not your fault."

Dean closed his eyes at the feeling of Amy's hand on his cheek.

"Does it hurt?"

"No, but it is tight. You may feel sad for me, but no woman alive is ever going to want to kiss me, to have me court them and to marry me. Look at my lips; they curl up at one end. How appealing is that?"

Amy moved her hand from his cheek, and just as he thought she would walk away she stood on tip-toe and kissed him on the mouth. Dean stood stock still, but as Amy didn't withdraw, he grabbed her hips and pulled her towards himself and then kissed her back. It was so long since anyone had willingly touched him that Dean wanted to continue kissing her forever. He pulled the band from her hair and ran his fingers through the silky strands. As the kiss continued, Dean pulled her shirt from where she had tucked it into her skirt, and his hands roved over her bare skin. He groaned when Amy stepped away, but the flushed face and dreamy eyes he saw on Amy said she had enjoyed the kiss as much as he did. When she collected her wits, Amy said, "You, Dean Turner, underestimate other women. I don't know who told you that you are undesirable, but that kiss proves they are wrong. And by the way, I don't want your damned *endurance* money."

Amy tucked in her shirt, redid her ponytail and headed for the door.

"I mustn't give Mrs Yardley anything more to hold against me."

When Amy left, Dean Turner lost all interest in chasing figures across the keyboard. Even under normal circumstances, the kiss was mesmerising, but considering they were at work and she had stormed into the room to chastise him, it made it more remarkable. Was Margot wrong? Her justification for cringing when he approached was that no woman would willingly associate with him unless it were for money. Was that what had happened between him and Amy? Did she think he was an easy target, and if she seduced him, she could access his wealth? There was no question about the validity of Amy's emotions when she kissed him. Dean remembered her flushed face as she attempted to put on her attire right before leaving the room, and he realised that he had had his hands in her hair and under her shirt, neither of which she complained about. He hoped Margot was wrong.

While Dean replayed their kiss and embrace, Amy was busy cursing herself. Sure, there was chemistry between them, but she didn't want to be that cliché of the secretary sleeping with the boss. He kissed like a starving man, and Amy wondered whether he and his fiancé had slept together since the accident. If she were less than welcoming, that would explain his lack of confidence and his assumption that no woman would ever want him. Did it matter what happened between them because wasn't she looking for another job when her agreement expired? Was Dean interested in more than a confidence-boosting fling? For the first time since she commenced work at Maddox Incorp, she left work without completing her tasks.

Mrs Yardley looked suspiciously at Amy when she returned to her desk; this warned her that the woman would do anything to discredit her. If the woman thought something untoward happened between Amy and Dean, she would go to HR to make a formal complaint. Amy vowed to keep her head down and ensure nothing more happened between her and Dean.

Amy's good intentions went out the window when Dean called her into his office early the following day. Her boss looked a little sleep-deprived and clicked his pen open and shut while gathering his courage.

"Amy, I need to have a personal conversation with you, but here is not the place. Can I take you out to dinner, and we can talk?"

Amy's eyes widened. Whatever Dean wanted to say had to be private, so she assumed it was about the kiss and what happened during that make-out session.

"I believe I owe you a meal, and while whatever I make won't be restaurant quality, I can assure you it will be tasty and edible. Why don't you come to my place, and then we don't risk being seen by anyone from work."

Dean nodded, and Amy gave him her address before leaving the room.

The workday seemed to drag on, and although she had no more interaction with Dean, she felt his presence. When she left work, Amy ran errands, including a stop at the supermarket for the ingredients needed to make her mum's lasagne recipe. With the food in the oven, Amy did a quick clean-up, showered, and dressed casually. Amy felt nervous despite having seen Dean daily for the past two months. Was he going to give her a private dressing down for her inappropriate actions? It would be hypocritical of him because he enjoyed the kiss as much as she did, and he was the one who got all handsy.

When Dean arrived, he carried a bottle of wine, which he handed to Amy.

"I wasn't sure what you were cooking, so I went with red wine."

"Come in. Red wine is perfect. I made a lasagne, and it was in the oven before I thought about food allergies."

"If it is as good as it smells, I'm glad I have no allergies."

"Come into the kitchen while I dish up. Do you want to slice the garlic bread? Once we get organised, I'll get you to pour the wine."

Seated at the table, Amy said, "I know you wanted to talk to me in private, but can we chat about other things before we get into heavy topics?"

"Sure, that makes sense."

Amy and Dean chatted and asked questions about each other. Not willing to give away her greatest mistake, Amy steered away from the topic of why she was working far away from her family. Dean talked about his family, although from the tone and what Dean said, Amy deduced that their relationship was full of expectations rather than the love she shared with her parents. Amy talked about her married sister and military brother affectionately, and Dean wished he had the same relationship with his siblings. He and his older brother competed, trying to beat each other whenever they had the same goals, and as the only girl in the family, his sister was pampered and spoiled.

Once they finished eating, Dean helped Amy clear the table and rinse the dishes for the dishwasher.

"Do you want more wine, coffee or tea? We could take our drinks into the lounge room."

Holding their drinks, tea for Amy and coffee for Dean, the two sat on the couch. Dean put his coffee on the low table and turned to Amy.

"I should start by apologising for mauling you the other day. That kiss is the first time I've been near a woman since the accident, and I lost my head."

Amy laughed. "Dean, I kissed you, so I should apologise. The kiss was supposed to show that women would want you, but it quickly became fiery. It's been a long while for me, too."

The two sat quietly for a few minutes, and Amy said, "Who told you that no woman would want you?"

"Have you seen any reports about the accident?"

"Yes. After I applied and saw you for the first time, I knew there was a story, so I Googled you."

"There is more to the story than the papers reported, but I didn't intend to divulge the reason for the accident except that Margot was drunk and the police breath-checked her, so there was no hiding that. Margot was the person who told me that no woman would be interested in me unless they wanted my money."

Amy's eyes widened. "So, you think...."

Tears welled in Amy's eyes, and she shot out of her chair.

"I think it is time you left. Rest assured, our kiss is the only one, and I will continue looking for employment elsewhere. Take the wine and get out."

Dean slammed the cork back into the bottle and strode to the door.

"Thank you for the meal."

Amy listened to the sound of the Dean gunning the powerful engine and slumped into a chair. She couldn't decide if she was angry with him or sad for him. His fiancé, the person who caused the crash, had so undermined Dean's confidence that he was looking for reasons, apart from attraction, to explain their kiss. Her outrage at his insinuation that she was after his money was so offensive that she couldn't express her anger except to shout all the obscene insults she knew. The thought of facing Dean tomorrow made her consider ringing in sick, but she knew that was a short-term solution.

CHAPTER 9

Amy greeted Kent as she walked through the foyer and tapped her foot while waiting for the lift. Today would be awkward, and Amy had dressed in her best outfit to give her confidence. When she walked into the office, Mrs Yardley scrutinised her outfit.

"Are you parading your goods, hoping to get a rise?"

Amy looked at the woman she had come to hate.

"Better than mutton dressed up as lamb."

The outraged scream had people running from all quarters.

"What the hell is going on in here?"

Amy glared at Dean.

"Nothing for you to worry about, Mr Turner."

Mrs Yardley stood and pointed at Amy.

"She just insulted me. She said I am mutton dressed up as lamb."

Amy heard some snickers from the on-lookers, but Dean glared at Amy.

"Do you think insulting your fellow workers is productive, Miss Benson?"

"I just called it like it is. Besides, when a co-worker has asked if I am showing off my goods to get a raise, I feel justified. I must remember to wear sweats and track shoes tomorrow so no one can make the comment she did."

Dean ran his hands through his hair and groaned. "This situation is untenable."

Amy stared at him. "I already told you I will quit if you give me a half-decent reference. You and Mrs Yardley can get together and say rude things about me when I'm gone."

Dean glared at the on-lookers.

"Get back to work, everybody. Mrs Yardley, you and Miss Benson must come into my office."

Dean sat behind his desk, all thoughts of shielding his face forgotten when dealing with the volatile situation he had.

"Mrs Yardley, why did you make that disparaging remark to Miss Benson?"

"I told you that her pretty face and trim figure caused Mr James to hire her even though she wasn't qualified. Look at her outfit today. The skirt is barely decent, and her top shows too much cleavage for a business such as ours. She would fit in better at a bar, not a respectable business."

Dean sighed. He privately thought Amy looked sensational.

"Miss Benson, what made you wear the outfit this morning? It is not the same as the other business attire I've seen."

Amy shook her head.

"I had a distressing evening last night where my date accused me of being a gold digger. I wore the outfit to boost my morale this morning, but if it offends, fire me or give me time to go home and change; either option suits me."

Dean flushed, his face turning pink at Amy's barb.

"Go home and change. You can make up the time at the end of the day."

As Amy walked away, Dean felt like a heel. He had eaten at her home, she had shared her hospitality, and he had indeed assumed she was a gold digger. Wearing the outfit she had that morning was a real fuck you decision, and sending her home to change only made his insinuation worse. Dragging his mind away from Amy, Dean looked at the woman who had instigated every dispute they had had since Amy arrived. Picking up the phone, Dean called Robert James to his office. As the officious little man entered the room, he scrutinised the man. Dean hadn't had any dealings with the HR man since the locked toilet debacle, and he tried to shelve his dislike of the man while they dealt with the problem of Mrs Yardley.

"Mr James, I have called you in as the Human Relations manager while I discuss Mrs Yardley's tenuous hold on her job. She has instigated three incidents aimed at discrediting Miss Benson, and I cannot think of a more constructive way of resolving the problem than firing one of the women. Have you any suggestions?"

Robert James frowned. "I am aware of two incidents. Did the third have something to do with the screams this morning?"

Dean explained, and the woman who had caused the commotion sat, blithely surveying the room. Robert James frowned.

"I assume we should fire the person who caused the problems, but can I suggest another solution? Why not separate the women? You have enough space in your office to house another desk, and if we put in a partition, Mrs Yardley could work there, and Miss Benson could stay in the main office. I assume the workload is the same as when Mrs Yardley decided she needed help. So, firing Miss Benson as the most recent hire doesn't make sense."

"Okay. Find Miss Benson's number, and I will ring her to tell her to take a paid day off and find a builder who can do the remodelling quickly. Mrs Yardley, you will have no assistance today, and considering Mr James has saved you from being fired, you can work late to complete your work."

Dean steeled himself to make the call when Robert James returned with Amy's number. When she answered, he heard her voice hesitate when she realised it was him.

"Mr Turner, have you rung to fire me?"

"No. Robert James had a suggestion that separates you from Mrs Yardley but allows you to keep your job. We are building a partition in my office; Mrs Yardley will work there, and you will remain in the main office. Take a paid day off; the partition will be in tomorrow, so today is better if you stay home. I'm sorry about the outfit."

"Whatever."

"Are you okay?"

"I'm fine."

Dean hung up and groaned. There were a thousand things he didn't understand about women, but one thing he did know was that a woman said she was fine; she was anything but okay.

Once the builder arrived and Dean explained what he needed, the man left with promises to return soon but said that the erection of a false wall would take a day or two. Dean asked Kent to assist him in moving Amy's computer into the break room as an interim measure, where she could work without seeing Mrs Yardley. Dean knew that Amy's temporary movement from the vicinity of his antagonistic personal assistant was the least of his worries. He had accused her of being after his money, and she had hit back the only way she could. Tonight, Dean knew he would need to visit her and apologise; otherwise, the only woman who could bear to look at him would leave the firm, and he would never see her again.

The workday seemed endless, and while he wanted to punish Mrs Yardley for her insult to Amy, he also punished himself because he couldn't leave until she did. Dean considered his options regarding Amy as he walked the woman from the building an hour after her usual finishing time. He could call her to discuss their problem, but he knew she would brush him off with her comments about being okay, so his only sensible option was to go to her home.

Amy looked through the peephole and groaned when she realised her visitor was Dean. Opening the door, she glared at him.

"What do you want?"

"To apologise? To beg your forgiveness? Please, Amy, let me in."

Amy hesitated for a moment and then stepped back so Dean could enter.

"Feel free to apologise, but I doubt I will forgive you for your comment."

"I'm sorry for assuming that what Margot said was true. The more I think about what happened between my ex-fiance and myself, the more I think her cutting comments were her trying to absolve herself of blame. You are nothing like her; I should have realised that initially. I'm sorry that I assumed you had an ulterior motive for the kiss."

Amy nodded.

"I want to know what happened between you and your ex-fiance that the papers didn't know about, not because I'm nosey, but because I want to understand where your lack of trust comes from. But first, have you eaten? Let's eat, and then, if you feel up to it, maybe you can enlighten me about your accident and its aftermath."

"I can do that, but then you have to explain why you applied for a job so far away from home and where you have been for the last four years. Your resume is blank for those years, and I don't believe you were hibernating."

"Okay, sure."

As Amy warmed up the casserole she had removed from the freezer that morning, Dean told her about the progress of the partition in his office.

"Do you want to be behind a closed door with Mrs Yardley? I don't want to sound like a bitch, but being shut off from the office will make it difficult to defend yourself if she decides to pay you back for not firing me."

"Damn, I hadn't thought of that. We might have to return to the drawing board and change the entry to my office and hers. I never realised the woman was so devious until she began to try to undermine you. I might set Robert James the task of finding a replacement."

"Replacing her is probably a good idea, but do you find something creepy about Robert James? The day he interviewed me, he called me "My dear" and then proceeded to look at my breasts instead of my face. As far as an HR manager goes, he has to be the worst example I've ever seen."

"Yeah, you're right. The man makes me uncomfortable, but pinpointing why is hard."

Once they finished dinner, Amy made them drinks, and they moved to the lounge room. Dean said, "Do you want to go first? I might take quite a while."

"My greatest mistake is not a brief story either."

As Amy told Dean about Lucas and what happened over the four years he studied as a doctor, she felt the anger and the unfairness of the situation return. Dean's outraged response to her tale made her feel marginally better, but nothing would remove the ingrained hurt. When she finished, he rose and hugged her.

"We need another drink, but let me get this one."

Amy sat and watched as Dean prepared the tea and coffee, and although she felt drained from retelling her story, she wanted to know what hardship had caused Dean to become so reclusive.

CHAPTER 10

When Dean handed Amy her drink, she held it in both hands, trying to ward off the chill that seeped into her soul whenever she thought about Lucas and her wasted years. Dean sat across from her and said, "It's my turn now, and this story has no happy ending either. Margot and I grew up together, and as we aged, we were often paired at social events because her parents and mine were in business together. As teenagers, we dated casually with the enthusiastic support of both parents. I had never met a girl who set my heart racing, and my parents expected me to marry well, so I decided Margot would do. When we announced our engagement, both Mothers began to discuss wedding plans, and Margot had definite ideas, so I let them go. All I wanted to do was turn up for the ceremony and say I do."

"Gosh, that's so terrible. What a horrid way to choose your life partner."

Dean shrugged. "After she got the ring on her finger, Margot became less affectionate and spent more time with her girlfriends. The time wasn't an issue because my Father pushed me hard to become a partner in his company. About a month before the wedding, a friend of mine had a housewarming party and despite her reluctance, Margot and I attended. We circulated for a while, and then, when someone turned on a football game, the men drifted into the lounge room and the women into the kitchen. Knowing that Margot had attended reluctantly, I decided we had done our duty and could leave."

Dean stopped his narration and took some sips from his coffee. Amy sat silently, instinctively aware that the next part of his recall would be the hardest. With a sigh, Dean continued.

"I went to the kitchen to collect her, but the women in the room thought we had left because they hadn't seen Margot for some time. Slightly peeved, I began a search of the house for her and, much to my surprise, tracked her to a bedroom with a man I didn't know. Both were in a state of undress, and the frantic kisses and the groping indicated that things were escalating. I would have discovered them in bed if I had arrived five minutes later. The man was embarrassed, but Margot was angry, and when she dressed, she swanned out of the house as though I had done something wrong. It was clear to me that she had too much to drink, and I suggested she let me drive, but she refused. It was then that I made the worst decision of my life. I got into the car, hoping to convince Margot to let me drive."

Amy shook her head. "You couldn't have known what would happen."

"Margot was screaming and raging at me, which was confusing since she was the person cheating. She was so incensed that she was weaving across the road, and I yelled at her to pull over, but she continued. The light turned red as she approached, and she kept going. Another car clipped our tail and pushed the front end into the path of a four-wheel drive. I had just enough time to throw myself across the console before the impact, and that's what saved my life. I could hear Margot screaming. Rescuers came and spoke to me, but I can't remember much until I woke in agony in the hospital. The doctors kept me drugged up for three or four days until they could reduce the painkillers slightly."

"Are you okay to continue?"

"Yes, let me finish this sorry tale. I had a broken hip, leg, collar bone and arm. I had broken ribs and some head injuries, but I had cuts on my face from the broken window. My parents visited, her parents visited, my siblings visited, and even friends visited, but Margot was too distressed after the accident to visit me."

"What a self-absorbed cow."

Dean nodded. "Six weeks after the accident, I started physio because the broken things needed to learn to work correctly. When I was allowed to go home, my darling fiancé finally visited me. I told her I expected fidelity even though we weren't a love match. Margot excused herself because she had too much to drink, and I told her she could do as she pleased because her anger and inebriation nearly killed me. My parents pressured me to forgive her, but I found it hard to do that.

She arrived one afternoon full of joy because she had found the best plastic surgeon in the country, according to her friends, and he would fix my facial scarring. I fought her suggestion, but when my parents and hers said that I should allow the man to erase the scars, I relented. Two botched operations later, the woman I was supposed to forgive and marry shuddered whenever I walked into the room and if I dared touch her, she just about swooned. I told my parents I couldn't forgive her for nearly killing me, for cheating on me and for ruining my face with her supposed top plastic surgeons. My Mother was disappointed, but my Father backed me, and I told Margot to cancel the already delayed wedding plans because we were not getting married. She said that I was so ugly she couldn't bear to look at me, and the only women ever likely to be interested would be after my money. I told her parents I was breaking off our relationship and left town."

Dean had his hands gripped tightly in his lap, and Amy moved to the arm of the chair. She slid her arms around his shoulders, and he turned his face to her chest and wept. Amy's anger with Dean had long since evaporated, but the tears and the anguish he showed while telling her his story broke her heart. Amy hated the smug socialite who nearly killed Dean and then made things so much worse by insisting he have plastic surgery. She wondered if his parents felt any guilt for supporting the plastic surgery.

As the tears stopped, Amy slid onto Dean's lap. He looked embarrassed, but Amy scolded him when he attempted to apologise for his emotional breakdown.

"Shush up, Dean Turner. My trouble pales compared to yours, and I often want to weep about my situation, so yours deserves a good cry now and then. If I'm ever unlucky enough to meet that woman, I will bitch-slap her for you."

" I would prefer it if you kissed me."

Amy turned in his arms and kissed his face before zeroing in on his mouth. Dean slid his hands into her hair and pulled Amy closer. He deepened the kiss, and Amy groaned with appreciation as the fiery kiss continued. Wanting to get closer, Amy straddled Dean's lap, and as she ground her hips against his erection, he groaned and pulled away.

"Unless you want to finish this in bed, you'd better stop wriggling on my lap."

Amy placed her hands on either side of Dean's face and smirked. "If you think I'm wriggling, I'm not doing it right. Do you think we can stop here now that I've felt how hard you are? Let's move to the bedroom because I want more of you."

Sliding off Dean's lap, Amy held out her hand to this man who had touched her heart and led him to her bedroom.

As Amy began to undo Dean's shirt buttons, he stilled her hand.

"Amy, there are nasty scars all over my torso. You might find it too uncomfortable with the light on."

Amy's mouth dropped open. "You honestly believe I want you groping in the dark. However, your look is fine by me. After all, my body isn't perfect."

Dean looked uncomfortable. "Margot said...."

"Don't ever speak that woman's name in my presence again. Just because someone else was too stupid to know what she was letting go doesn't mean I need to hear about it. You sound like an unwilling virgin."

She looked down at his tented pants and said, "It looks like you might have the equipment to do the job, so more action, less talk."

Dean laughed before grabbing her and throwing her on the bed. He followed her down, and the kissing and touching reached an all-time high before Dean began peeling off Amy's clothes.

Once Amy was naked, Dean shook his head in wonder. He couldn't take his eyes off her tight, high breasts with their pink areolas and tight nipples. Her skin was flushed, and as his eyes slid downwards, he noticed her trim waist and generous hips. Amy squirmed at his perusal and silence.

"Maybe we should have done this in the dark."

Dean shook his head. "You are so gorgeous, and I'm sorry if I'm staring, but I don't think I've ever seen anything more perfect."

"Your clothes need to come off too."

Amy sat up and resumed unbuttoning his shirt. When she parted the sides, she stared at his torso and laughed.

"You mentioned the scars but failed to mention the six-pack and the pectoral muscles."

Amy ran her hands along his arms and across his chest before sliding them to the waistband of his dress pants. She undid the top button before sliding the zip open, and when her hand delved into his tight underwear, he groaned as she released his erection and wrapped her hands around his cock..When Dean groaned, Amy saw her companion gritting his teeth. She removed her hands and sat back.

"I'm sorry. Was I hurting you?"

"God, no, but it's been so long. I might come before we get started if you keep touching me."

"Let me take the edge off if you aren't a once-a-night lover."

Amy slid back towards Dean and ran her tongue across the top of his cock before sliding it into her mouth, where she hollowed her cheeks and began to suck. The groans Dean made spurred her on, and it wasn't long before he stuttered,

"You have to stop. Amy. I can't hold on."

Amy continued her ministrations, and seconds later, she was swallowing the spurts of come that filled her mouth.

When she pulled away, Dean lay on the bed, spent from his first sexual encounter with anyone but his hand in two years. He pulled Amy towards himself and wrapped his arms around her.

"Give me a few minutes, and I'll take care of you. Do you have any condoms?"

"No, because I didn't have a boyfriend after Lucas. I am on the pill, and I got tested after I discovered Lucas was cheating, so I'm clean."

"I'm clean too. It seems our cheating exes did us a favour."

CHAPTER 11

That night was the first of many. While Dean and Amy remained professional at work and discrete in public, they spent many hours together. Amy suggested Dean wear a mask when out in public, and they ventured to places he hadn't been confident about visiting. Given the information beforehand, Amy found that wait staff placed them in booths away from the middle of the restaurant, and no one could see Dean's face in the dark at movie theatres.

Dean had eaten many meals at Amy's place and spent many nights, so when he arrived for dinner one night, she had a packed overnight bag standing at the door.

Dean gave her an enquiring look and said, "Are you going somewhere?"

"Yes, to your place, assuming you don't sleep on a park bench. I want to see where you live. We can order take-away. But I want to spend the night at your house."

"It's not as cosy as your place."

"You forget this house is not my place, but I want to spend the night at your home."

Dean's home was an apartment in a block of condominiums. The place looked like Dean showered and slept but never spent much time there. A large dining room table cluttered with documents and a laptop showed Dean worked at home. There were no photos of family or friends and no homey touches. Amy surveyed the room and said, "Your decorator was into minimalist décor I see."

Dean grinned. "I've never needed more, and as I have no visitors, it didn't seem worth fixing the place up."

After that first visit to Dean's home, they spent time in both places. Dean gave Abby a key to meet him at home if she finished work before he did. Slowly, as time went on, Amy added some homey touches and the day Dean entered to find cushions on the couch, he laughed. What was this woman doing to him? Dean realised he felt happy, which he hadn't felt in a long time. Amy had changed his life with her acceptance of his damaged face and scarred body, and she had disproved Margot's barb that only a woman interested in money would suffer looking at his face.

Amy was humming to herself as she prepared dinner when the phone rang. It surprised Amy that Dean had a landline, but she assumed it was easier to do business deals when the phone didn't continually drop out. Amy ignored the phone, thinking that whoever it was would get the message that Dean wasn't home, but after it rang twice more, she decided she should answer the call. Could it be Dean ringing to tell her he was running late? Wiping her hands on the teatowel, Amy picked up the receiver. Before she could speak, a woman's voice said, "About time you answered. I rang three times because I wanted to talk to you."

Amy raised an eyebrow at the pushy woman and said, "If you rang to talk to Dean, he isn't home yet. Can I take a message?"

The woman's voice became shrill as she demanded, "Who are you, and why are you answering my fiancé's phone?"

Before she could answer, she heard a key in the door, and Dean walked in.

"Hi, sweetheart, what's with the phone?"

The woman's shrill voice continued to yell threats from the phone, and Amy said, "The woman said she is your fiancé and needs to talk to you."

Dean growled and grabbed the phone. As Amy prepared to leave the room to give Dean privacy, he grabbed her hand and pulled her close. Speaking into the handset, Dean said, "I am not your fiancé and never will be again, so I would appreciate it if you would stop using that false title. What do you want?"

"Who is the woman, and why is she answering your phone?"

"You have no right to ask any of those questions, but the woman is my girlfriend, and she has a key to my place. But that's not why you rang, so why are you bothering me?"

"It's time for you to come home and do your duty. We should have married twelve months ago."

Dean chuckled, but there was no joy associated with the noise. "You seem to forget; thanks to you, I am so scared you can't bear to look at me. You cheated on me, and you almost killed me. I made it clear before I left town that you and I are not getting married. How did you get my number?"

"Your Mother gave me the number because she is disappointed that the wedding didn't go through."

"It seems like I will have to change my phone number. Don't call again; we have nothing to discuss."

Dean slammed down the phone; the unwanted call dissipated his good mood. As he walked towards the kitchen, the phone began to ring again, and Amy turned, pulled out the plug and moved to pour a glass of wine for Dean. Skulling the drink in one go, Dean poured another glass of wine. Amy moved closer, took the glass from his hand and wrapped her arms around her upset boyfriend. They stayed together, giving and receiving comfort for many minutes. Neither of them talked until Amy dished their meal.

"I might have to go home to make them understand that the marriage is not happening."

Dean ran his hands through his hair in frustration. "Why is it so difficult to understand that I won't marry the woman? She cheated on me, she nearly killed me, and she can't even look at me. Doesn't anyone care if I'm happy or not? Pulling the doing my duty thing is a dirty trick, and while it makes me feel guilty, it doesn't convince me that I should marry the tramp."

Dean was quiet for the remainder of the evening, and even though she brought a bag, intending to stay the night, she said, "Do you want me to go home?"

Dean nodded. "Yeah, I'm in too bad a mood to be very pleasant. Give me the weekend to sort out my life, and I'll see you on Monday."

Amy kissed Dean on the cheek and walked away. As she drove towards her place, Amy wondered how strong Dean's sense of duty was and if he would sacrifice his life for his family. Amy felt a sense of foreboding. She had stayed single ever since the betrayal by Lucas, and Dean was the first man she let herself care about for years. Despite trying to harden her heart against developing feelings for another man, Amy had gone and fallen in love with Dean. He had the power to break her heart, and Amy wondered if she could survive another heartbreak caused by a man.

As Dean watched Amy leave, he regretted that he had told her to go. He needed her warmth and understanding but was afraid he would say something that offended her. The phone call from Margot had scrambled his brain. Here he was, in a place far away, with a woman he had come to care about, and Margot was once again ruining his life.

Dean shook his head; he wouldn't let the witch ruin the best relationship he had ever experienced. Amy was so kind and caring that he lost his inhibitions when she was around. She didn't care what he looked like in private and had suggested using a mask when they went out. After the COVID-19 epidemic, it wasn't unusual to see people wearing masks, so his use of one didn't cause concern or curiosity.

Margot's comment about him doing his duty made him feel ill. He couldn't imagine being married to the woman who cheated on him, who nearly killed him and then abandoned him as he lay in hospital fighting for his life. Dean knew he'd have to fly home to speak to his parents, Margot, and her parents. After all that had happened, his parents couldn't believe he should marry Margot.

Dragging himself from the chair he had slumped in after the phone call, he opened his laptop and booked a flight for the first thing in the morning. He would need to contact his cousin Mike to supervise the business while he was away. Before packing his suitcases, Dean wrote a letter to Amy, explaining where he was and assuring her that he wanted to sort out the rubbish between him and Margot.

CHAPTER 12

Dean

The flight was bumpy, with air turbulence causing nervous passengers to squeal when the plane dropped and rose as they crossed the mountains. The seat belt light remained on for the entire flight, so the passengers sighed with relief when the plane touched down. Dean strode across the terminal to collect his bags and scanned the concourse for the driver of the car he ordered. Thankfully, the driver wasn't chatty, and Dean tried to make a plan of attack. He would spend the night at a motel and arrive at his parents' house to discuss his problem tomorrow.

Dean ordered room service and wondered if he should call Amy. With regret, he shelved the idea; he needed to focus on the fucked-up situation here rather than pinning for the woman he left in West Wynton. The following day, dressed in jeans and a sweatshirt, Dean took a taxi to his parents' house. His unexpected arrival caused curiosity, but it was nice to enter a home where the occupants didn't cringe when they saw his face. His Mother kissed him, and his Father gave him a backslap. Dean pushed the purpose of his visit aside as he caught up on what his parents and siblings were doing.

Eventually, his dad said, "As lovely as it is to see you, there must be a purpose to your visit because it seems you made a last-minute decision."

Dean nodded his agreement. "When I took over Maddox Industries, I was so busy that I became reclusive. I went to work, drove home, had a takeaway meal and went to bed. It was the same day after day until the HR manager hired an assistant for my PA. The girl was in her twenties, pretty with a neat figure, and my PA hated her.

She thought of ways to get the woman fired, and I was constantly putting out fires. The assistant stormed into my office one day, shaking her payslip at me. Amy was outraged that I paid the people who had face-to-face contact with me a small weekly bonus for their distress. She refused the payment and said if my staff were so weak, I ought to fire them and hire more thoughtful, accepting people."

Bill Turner nodded his head. "I believe I would like the young lady you are describing."

"I'm glad because Amy and I started dating after that encounter. We have been very discrete, and I don't believe anyone else has realised. I know office romances can end in tragedy, but I believe this will end in a marriage if I have my way."

Dean watched the accepting nod of his Father and the pinched expression on his Mother's face. Neither parent

"What about your duty to the family? Margot is the person you would have married if the accident hadn't happened, and I'm sure you could work out your differences."

Despite his desire to shout at his Mother, Dean took a few calming breaths and said, "So, to honour a family tradition, you want me to spend the rest of my days unhappy? You want me to marry a woman I hate and can't forgive to honour some outdated sense of duty?"

His Mother flushed, but she said, "You and Margot seemed to get on fine when you got engaged."

"I was never overly fond of Margot, and now that I've met Amy, I realise it would be a crime to marry a woman I don't like to appease my family. You are right, mum. I was agreeable to marry Margot, but she gave me a taste of what married life would be like if we married, and I don't want to live my life like that."

"I don't understand. Margot says she still loves you and will become accustomed to your face in time."

Flicking his eyes towards his Father Dean, he said, "Does she not know what happened?"

His Father shook his head. "Tony Dimitrio asked me to keep the details quiet because it could ruin his daughter's reputation."

"So, I must live a miserable life to protect her reputation. The man never asked me, so I intend to tell mum about that night."

As Dean began his recitation, he watched as his Mother's face paled, and by the time he finished telling her about the hospital and rehab, she was visibly upset.

"Mum, I hate the woman, and no threat or amount of honour could convince me to marry her. I came to help cancel the preparations still in place and let the Dimitrio family know that the tradition ends here."

Bill Turner nodded his head. "I agree that you shouldn't marry the little hussy. The family spoiled her, so she believes she can do whatever she wants without repercussions. I, for one, would not condemn you to a miserable marriage."

Mary Turner sighed. "I understand your refusal to marry her now that I know the full story. Perhaps we should visit tomorrow and provide a united front. Once we sort this problem out, you had better let us meet the girl who stole your heart."

Dean and his parents arrived at the Dimitrios house for morning tea the following day. Dean was confident that if they had accepted an invitation for dinner, Margot would have excused herself if she had to look at him before the meal ended. The Turner and Dimitrio families exchanged greetings, and once the small talk ended, Maria Dimitrio said, "I assume you have come to discuss the wedding."

Dean nodded. "Yes, you are correct, but what you assume I want to discuss is incorrect. I have come to tell you there will be no wedding between Margot and me, and I've come to help cancel the bookings and attempt to get some refunds."

Maria Dimitrio gasped, and Tony growled.

"You will do your duty, son."

"With respect, sir, I am not doing my duty by marrying your daughter. I hate her for what she did to me, and if she is so enamoured with me, where is she? Here we are discussing the wedding, and she isn't here."

Tony Dimitrio stood, and Bill Turner stood as he approached Dean with his fists clenched.

"Leave him alone, Tony. My son agreed to enter a loveless marriage to fulfil his duty, but even you can't believe after what your daughter did that he should marry her."

Tony stood and glared at the Turner men, but Maria broke the silence.

"You shouldn't hold a grudge; what happened was an accident."

Mary, who hadn't spoken since they entered the room, said, " Maria, our husbands didn't tell us the full story about what led to the accident and its aftermath."

When the Turner family left, Dean prayed that the episode was over. He wanted to go home to West Wynton, but having committed to helping dismantle the wedding preparations, he had to spend another week here. The following week flew past as Dean and his Mother unwound the arrangements for the wedding. After such a long delay, it took some smooth talking to get refunds, but even without the money, Dean was adamant about cancelling the plans.

After meeting with the wedding planner, Dean arrived at his parents' home to discover unknown cars parked in the driveway. As Dean entered the house, he was surprised at the number of voices he heard, and as he made his way to the kitchen, some of the voices became clearer. He smiled as he entered the kitchen and found his brother, sister and brother-in-law at the table.

"What are you lot doing here?" Dean asked.

Kate, his sister, said, "Mum called us and said you were here cancelling wedding plans and trying to get refunds, so we had to come and congratulate you on ditching that spoiled brat you were supposed to marry. Well done, bro!"

Dean wanted to stay and enjoy his family's company, so he texted Amy to let her know he would be away a little longer. As he told his sibling about Amy, Dean glowed as he described her, and while his Mother was sad about the end of a tradition, she could see that the woman he spoke of made him happy.

CHAPTER 13

Amy

Dean didn't contact Amy over the weekend, and as they usually texted one another a few times a day about their arrangements for the night, his silence concerned her. Dean had said he would see her on Monday, so would sending him a text message seem needy? With no answers to her questions, Amy turned her attention to cleaning the house from top to bottom. While she intended to leave the home spotless for the homeowners, cleaning today gave her something to concentrate on. On Sunday, with no texts or messages from Dean, Amy ran through the job options on her Facebook page. If Dean came back and said he was doing his duty and marrying the shrew, Amy would take her broken heart to another business so that she didn't have to see the man she loved with a woman he disliked.

On Monday morning, Amy entered the building and greeted Kent.

"Miss Benson, good morning. I want to inform you that Mr Turner has taken leave, and some relative will run the business while he's away."

Amy felt sick; the knowledge that Dean had left without letting her know was like a stab in the heart. Concealing her feelings was hard, but she smiled and nodded her head. She thought the look Kent gave her was sympathetic, but kindness in any form would result in a torrent of tears, so it was best to cut any conversation short. When Amy entered the office, the place was in uproar. People milled around the break room and the hallways, speculating on the reason for the sudden CEO change. They gossiped about why Dean had left, and the suggestions veered from the absurd to the offensive. Amy poured a cup of tea and headed to her room; at least there, she could be alone and if she crossed paths with Mrs Yardley, she and Amy rarely spoke.

Dean's office door opened, and a man stepped out. He was shorter than Dean and had a swarthy complexion and black hair. He stopped before her desk and smirked at her.

"So, you are my assistant. I'm sure we'll get to know each other well."

Amy's heart sank. This man would not be easy to work for, and he gave off a creepy feeling that made Amy's heart sink. Keeping calm, she said, "Actually, Mrs Yardley is your assistant, and I am her assistant, so I don't imagine we will have much to do with each other."

The man grinned and said, "Don't be too sure about that."

With that last suggestive comment, he called the staff to order and addressed them, introducing himself and explaining that Dean had taken personal leave.

Once everyone returned to their desks and order was restored, The buzzer on her desk sounded, and she answered the call.

"Miss Benson, will you come to my office, please."

Amy felt anxious about meeting Mike Preston in his office and vowed to apply for other jobs after work today. When Amy entered the office, the man didn't look at her but kept his head bent and his eyes focused on the computer screen. She fidgeted as her temper rose. He used this ploy to intimidate her, and she wasn't in the mood to play power games with this man. Amy turned to walk away, and he barked at her to stay put. Amy swung around and said, "It's clear you are busy. I can come back later."

Mike Preston rose from his seat and laughed.

"I can see why Dean hired you. He always liked a challenge."

"Mr Turner did not hire me; his PR manager Robert James hired me."

"Not according to Mrs Yardley."

Amy shook her head in disgust. "Mrs Yardley is a bitter, middle-aged woman who does not want to age gracefully. If you and Mr Turner had done a proper handover, you would know she had caused so much trouble that builders constructed the wall in this office so I didn't have to sit in the same room as her. Did you call me here for anything, or did you want to bait me?"

"I asked you to come here to inform you that Dean will be gone for about a month. He and his fiancé have set a date, and after the wedding, he has booked a week in Hawaii for their honeymoon."

Amy felt sick. Her assumption that he might buckle due to family pressure was correct. She looked at the hateful man who was gleefully shattering her dreams."He hates that woman. Why would he marry her?"

"I doubt that is any of your business. But we have business of our own. Dean said you were a pretty good lay, and he thought you might accommodate me with some sexual favours."

Amy gasped. Disbelief and outrage wared within her. She glared at the man who had gleefully reported the worst news of her life and sneered.

"There is no way in hell that I will accommodate you. You are a foul, disgusting man, and I can't believe Dean thought you were fit to run his company."

As Amy turned to storm away, Mike Preston grabbed her arm. She yanked her arm, attempting to free herself, and when she screamed, he backhanded her and pushed her against the wall. Dear God, the man was going to rape her. He tore at her shirt, and once the material parted, he pulled her bra down past her breasts so they were completely exposed. Slapping and whimpering, Amy tried to free herself, and her last effort was to try to knee him in the groin. Her aim was accurate, and the man crumpled to the ground as Amy ran for the door. She pushed her bra into place and attempted to hold the torn sections of her shirt together.

Racing through the building, she saw the shocked faces of her workmates. When she staggered into the entryway, the expression on Kent's face undid her. Amy burst into tears, and Kent pulled her into his office and comforted her. As the tears finally stopped, he said, "Sit there while I call the police."

"No, please don't. Mike Preston will only spin a story about me propositioning him, and Mrs Yardley will back him, even though she wasn't in the room."

Kent watched Amy with concern. "Let me find a shirt for you to wear. I understand why you are hesitant to report this, but go to the hospital and have them check your face."

Amy agreed, and when Kent handed her a shirt, she disappeared into the ladies' room to make repairs to her appearance. Hunting through her handbag, she pulled out a lipstick that she rarely wore and wrote a message on the mirror.

Beware! Mike Preston is a sexual predator.

Satisfied with her message, she returned to Kent's office.

Her face ached, and her head throbbed, but she needed to let Kent know she would be okay.

"Thank you, Kent. It's been a pleasure to know you. As you can guess, I won't be back."

"Mr Turner will be sad to know you've left.

Tears welled in her eyes as she said, "I thought he loved me, but he's gone home to do his duty and marry a woman he hates."

Kent looked distressed as Amy walked away and wondered why Dean Turner would disregard this good woman in favour of doing his duty. Although he didn't know what prompted Amy's assault, Kent was worried. Was the assault directed at Amy, or would the other women in the office be at risk? How could Dean ask a man like Mike Preston to oversee his business when it was clear that the man was not honourable? Kent was concerned for Amy. He doubted that she would go to the hospital to have her face checked and had only said she would to appease him. The comments she made about Dean affirmed his suspicion that there was something more between his boss and the young employee, and whatever choice Dean had made caused her heartbreak. If Dean were here now, he would shake the man until his teeth rattled.

CHAPTER 14

Amy slumped down on the couch, and a mixture of grief and disbelief assailed her. How could Dean walk away without so much as a note or message? Did their time together mean nothing? She believed him when he said he hated Margot, but why would he throw away their relationship to pander to his parent's wishes? Dean told her that his Father understood why he wouldn't marry Margot, but had the man changed his mind? Why would parents want their child to marry a woman who was entirely unsuitable and one who would make their son miserable?

Amy pulled out her phone and punched in Dean's number. She held her breath as the phone rang and smiled when someone picked it up. Unfortunately, the person who answered the phone was the shrew, Margot.

"I would like to speak to Dean."

The woman laughed. "Not likely. Why do you think I pinched his phone? I won't have you ruining my plans."

"You don't love him and can't even look at him. He will be miserable married to you; let him go."

"The only one going is you."

The woman hung up the phone, and Amy's tears flowed again.

When the phone rang again, Amy anxiously grabbed it, but the unknown number made her frown. Still, Dean might be on another device other than his, so she answered the call cautiously.

"Hello, Amy. This is Lorraine Finney here."

"Ah, hello, Mrs Finney. How can I help you?"

Amy heard the other woman sigh, and she said, "Henry has had a bit of a turn, and the doctor we saw advised us to return home and seek a cardiologist in our area. We agreed on you house sitting for six months, but we must come home now, not in another few months. Henry and I are happy for you to remain our guest for the remainder of the time if that suits you."

Amy realised this change in plans was a blessing in disguise. Nothing held her here; she would never return to Maddox Industries, and her lover was marrying another woman so she could vacate immediately.

"Mrs Finney, my job has fallen through and with nothing in town holding me, I can vacate the place within the next day or two."

Amy and Lorraine Finney discussed handing over the keys and replacing the food the homeowner had left initially for Amy. After sorting the issues to their satisfaction, Amy bid the homeowner goodbye, wished her husband well and ended the call. She spent the remainder of the day folding clothes to pack in her suitcases and locating boxes for toiletries, books, and nick-nacks. Early the following day, Amy placed the house keys in the key safe and headed for home.

Amy drove on autopilot as memories of her time with Dean tortured her. No matter how often she looked back for red flags, she couldn't find anything that caused her to believe he would leave her to fulfil his duty to his parents. Every time the subject arose, he was adamant that the woman who was supposed to be his wife was a lying, cheating hussy. Undoubtedly, the fact that his supposed fiancé couldn't look at him without cringing with disgust ought to make his parents aware of the sacrifice they were asking Dean to make.

That night, Amy slept at a cosy bed and breakfast and was on the road bright and early. She turned the radio on, hoping that the mindless chatter of the radio hosts would distract her from memories of Dean. When Lucas cheated on her, Amy had long since lost her girlish infatuation for him, and the blow he dealt her did not involve heartache, just fury at his backflip. But Dean had worked his way into her heart, so she felt heartbroken, confused and sad this time. If he had left her to fulfil his parents' wishes, she knew that his life with the trollop would be one of pain and suffering.

Amy was hungry; breakfast was a long time ago, and while she wanted to finish this trip, she knew she should stop, rest and eat. As she drove through Brighten, she kept her eyes on the road, trying to scan places that served food. A large sign for the Food Place came up, and Amy turned into the small parking lot. She hoped the food was edible but needed a cup of tea and a short break.

When she walked into the café, the perky blond woman behind the counter greeted her and asked if she was to eat in or take away. The woman's scrutiny made Amy realise that she probably sported a significant bruise on her cheek, and she reached up to finger the tender skin. With sympathy, the woman asked if Amy needed help, and Amy assured her that she had left the man who gave her the bruise and was going home to her parents. Amy ordered the tea she desperately wanted and a pancake with ice cream and maple syrup. Satisfied with Amy's explanation, the server chatted with Amy as she ate, and for the first time since Dean sent her home on Friday, she felt content. Once Amy left Brighten, she knew the roads well, and the familiar landmarks passed quickly. As she pulled into her parent's driveway way, Amy felt the tears well as she imagined her parents' reaction to the bruise on her face.

When her Mother opened the door, her eyes widened, and then she said, "Oh, my goodness, Amy, what happened to your face."

Amy sighed. "It's a long story and a bit unoriginal, I'm afraid. Can I come in?"

Flustered, Ruth Benson moved away from the door and followed her daughter as she walked to the kitchen. Amy slumped on a kitchen chair and said, "Explain why my taste in men is so bad."

"If he hit you and gave you that bruise, I have to agree that your taste in men is lacking."

"No, he didn't."

Ruth Benson turned the kettle on and said, "Once we have our drinks, you must tell me everything. Including why you are here on a work day."

With her drink on the table in front of her, Amy began to tell her mother about Dean, the horrid job, and the events of the last few days. Her tears returned as she talked about Dean, and she sobbed as he tried to continue with her story. Her Mother hugged Amy as she cried, and it reminded her of holding Dean when he told her about his accident.

"When Lucas lied and refused to fulfil his part of the bargain, you were upset, angry and crushed. This time, though, you are heartbroken and confused. You were in love with this man, weren't you?"

Amy nodded. "I thought he felt the same, but I must have seen affection that wasn't there."

"Do you believe that he told the other man you would provide sexual favours?"

"No. Dean may have walked away without telling me, but despite how crushed I feel, I know he is a decent man. He mightn't loved me like I love him, but he would never cheapen what we had by making a disgusting comment about me being a good lay. That is all on Mike Preston."

"What are you going to do now? It seems like we are back where we were when Lucas cheated you out of university."

"Give me a week or two to get my mind in order, and I'll re-evaluate my options then."

Amy had to tell her Father what happened, and although she attempted to remain stoic, the tears she was battling flowed over. Her Father wanted to visit Mike Preston to punch him in the face, but Amy convinced him it would achieve nothing.

After a week of grieving and thinking, Amy came up with a plan for revenge and to set her life on track, but first came the revenge. A phone call to the police station at West Wynton was her first job. Talking to the receptionist at the station was only the beginning of her complicated explanation. Once the receptionist transferred her, Amy introduced herself to the officer named Craig Butcher.

"Hello, Officer Butcher; I wish to discuss a sexual assault that happened to me recently."

"Miss Beson, are you reporting the crime?"

"No, because once you begin to investigate, the man in question will say I propositioned him, and my arch-enemy at the office will collaborate on his story, even though she wasn't present at the attack."

"Could I have details? Despite your reluctance to report, I assume you have a plan or reason for calling."

"The business is Maddox Industries, and the CEO is Dean Turner. Mr Turner took personal leave and placed his cousin, Mike Preston, in charge. Within the first hour of being in charge, he called me into his office and said he expected the same sexual favours as his cousin had received. I was in a relationship with Dean Turner; there was nothing tawdry about our relationship. When I refused Mike Preston, he attacked me. I screamed, and he backhanded me. I only escaped when I used my knee in his groin. The doorman, Kent, wanted me to report the incident, but knowing how the man and my enemy would rewrite the incident, I didn't want to. Kent cleaned me up, found a shirt to replace the torn one I was wearing, and after I left a note for other women in the business, I left."

"So the doorman can collaborate on what you are saying?"

"Yes, he can."

"So what do you want me to do with this information?

"I want you to know that there is something off about that workplace. The HR man has the women's toilets locked, and anyone wanting to use the facilities has to ask for the key and listen to his lecture about wasting company time. I think Mr James has cameras in the toilets and hand washing area, which he loads onto his computer. I believe Mike Preston has already pressured women into sexual favours thing with the threat of him firing them if they don't comply. There are women there who desperately need their jobs, and I'd hate them to have to succumb to the man's advances rather than lose their jobs."

"I'm at a loss to know what to say."

"Please check my story with Kent, but if you are going to investigate the place, you need to tell Kent not to announce you. Robert James sits at his computer all day, so if you aren't sneaky and remove him from his office, he may be able to wipe his videos before you get there."

"Why are you doing this?"

"Because it is the right thing to do. I don't want other women to undergo the same trauma I did."

"Well, Miss Benson, I will be in touch."

Ruth Benson, who was in the kitchen as her daughter talked to Officer Butcher, smiled when Amy hung up.

"That was a brave thing you did, Amy, and I'm proud of you."

Amy and her Mother hugged, and as she pulled away from her Mother's arms, Amy said, "I've just started. I'm looking for a female solicitor to see if I have a case to claim for what Lucas stole from me. I have a folder of receipts from his course and books, equipment, scrubs, lab coats, and so much more."

"Let me ring Callie Ryan. She raved about the woman she used when she had a tussle with her brother over her deceased Mother's estate."

CHAPTER 15

The woman behind the desk rose, her smile genuine, and Amy liked her immediately.

"Have a set, Amy and tell me how I can help you."

Fifteen minutes later, Danni Grant said, "I'm astounded. After sponging off you for four years, the man had the nerve to buy an engagement ring for another woman with your money?"

"I have receipts for the medical and university expenses and requested a printout of my rental record. The utility bills are in my email. I also have an itemised document for the fuel card we used. Each time one of us filled up, the receipt showed the vehicle involved. The food bills were weekly, and I didn't keep a record, although the bill was around two hundred dollars weekly for the first few years."

"Tell me about the shared bills."

"Lucas lived at the flat with me for the first two years, but in the third, he sometimes slept at the hospital, but I always knew when he had slept the night because he never made the bed and left his laundry for me to do. I think I ironed a thousand pairs of scrubs and about half that many lab coats during our association. Towards the end of the fourth year, he said he was too tired to come home, but I believe he was wooing his rich girlfriend during those months."

"You, Miss Benson, have been royally screwed. I will help you to get your money. Leave your documentation with me, and I'll have Monica split the communal bills and tally the costs. What is the doctor's name?"

"Lucas McCann."

"We'll track him down and send him a nice letter to remind him of his responsibilities."

Two weeks later, Amy received a call from Officer Butcher.

"Miss Benson, I'm sorry I've taken two weeks to get back to you, but your suspicions about Robert James and the temporary CEO were correct. I talked to the doorman, Kent, and he verified your account of the assault. We found fifteen hidden cameras in the ladies' room, and you were correct when you suggested he might have videos on his computer. Our friend Mike Preston had pressured women into having sex with them after threatening them with termination. We charged both men with a range of crimes, from sexual assault and coercion to other sex-related offences. Your female fellow workers owe you a vote of thanks. A woman named Kelly told us about your warning written in lipstick in the toilets downstairs, and it helped some women avoid the man."

"I'm glad you have caught both men. You might have to contact the CEO to tell him his business is falling apart."

"Yes, we've been onto him, and he will be returning next week to deal with the fallout."

When Amy told her parents about Officer Butler's call, they were pleased that while Amy didn't charge Mike Preston with attempted rape, he got his comeuppance anyway. In the privacy of her bedroom, Amy wondered what Dean would do now that his company was embroiled in a scandal. Cleaning up an image after such a public takedown was a hard ask, but she reminded herself of what Officer Butler had told her; the women were now safe and extremely grateful, so she had achieved her aim.

Dean

Dean's holiday had ended when he received a call from Officer Butler regarding the investigation into his company. The officer said he was alerted to the problems by a former employee, and the woman's suspicion had proved accurate. After the phone call, Dean booked the next flight home, and his parents and sibling wished him the best but reiterated their desire to meet Amy.

Dean approached his office with trepidation. He talked to Kent immediately after the call from the police officer and gave the staff paid time off until today. As he entered the foyer, Kent gave him a sympathetic look.

"A bad business, Mr Turner."

Dean shook his head. "Robert James always made me feel uncomfortable, but I never suspected there was something criminal about him. But what would I know, considering I left a sexual predator in charge of a business that females primarily staff."

Kent shook his head as Dean walked to the elevator. When Dean arrived in his office, the mood was sombre, and Dean wasted no time greeting the staff, so he asked them to assemble in the break room. Besides how nervous the female staff looked, he noticed that Amy was not among those gathered in the room.

"Where is Miss Benson?"

Most staff looked uncomfortable, but Mrs Yardley was the first to speak. She cackled as she said, "The trollop has left. Miss Benson hit on the new boss and got more than she bargained for. When he accepted her offer, the slut raced out of there, wailing and snivelling. Serve herself right, I say. I told you she only got the job because of her looks, and she tried to get a promotion by offering sexual favours. It's probably lucky that you're so ugly that she didn't hit on you, Mr Turner."

A collective gasp was the response to the woman's comment, and Dean paled as he watched the woman reveal what had happened in his absence.

"Mrs Yardley, I may be ugly on the outside, but you are not only ugly on the outside, but on the inside as well. The police charged Mike Preston with sexual assault, but while I have no intention of naming his victims, I know that you weren't one of them. Does that tell you something? We have no human relations officer, so I don't need to justify my decisions. Pack your belongings; you are fired."

Despite the woman's pleas and apologies, Dean locked his gaze on a woman seated at the end of the table and said,

"Tiffany, will you ring Kent to escort Mrs Yardley from the building? He needs to accompany her because I believe she will sabotage our work if we leave her alone.

Once Kent left with the woman in tow, Dean said, "I need a temporary PA. Does anyone want to put their hand up for that? Unless one of you fellows wants the job, I will ask the temp to work in the open office where Miss Benson did."

When a woman asked to do the job, Dean sent her and a male colleague to Mrs Yardley's office to access files on her computer that were not on Amy's. As Dean settled himself in his office, the question of Amy's whereabouts plagued him. Before he could delve further, his temp called him to Mrs Yardleys office.

"Look at this, Mr Turner."

Dean watched in fascination as the temp pulled up file after file that contained games, quizzes, crosswords, action games and some soft porn sites.

"Oh, my God. Miss Benson was right. When Mrs Yardley complained about her workload at one stage, Miss Benson said the woman spent all day banging keys but never seemed to achieve anything. Now I know why. Transfer anything useful to the computer in the other room, and then I'll send Travis to do a factory clean on that computer."

Dean shook his head as he once again resumed his seat at his desk. Not only did he need a human relations officer, but unless his temp wanted the job permanently, he needed to replace Mrs Yardley. Dean wondered what Mike had achieved while he was here. Did the man do any worthwhile work, or did he spend his time preying on women? Dean opened the top drawer where he kept his planner, and his eyes widened as he discovered the letter he had written to Amy. By the neat cut, it appeared that someone had used a paper knife to slit the envelope. Why was the letter in the top drawer? With a sick realisation, it occurred to him that while Mike opened the letter, he had not given it to Amy. Dean's heart sank. After sending her home the night Margot called, without reading the letter, Amy would believe he had deserted her. Was Amy, the former employee Officer Butler said, called in the police? He wondered when she left and how angry she was. Dean quickly called Kent and asked him to come to his office.

When Kent arrived, Dean waved him into the opposite chair and said, "Do you know why Amy left? When did she leave, and was she the person who called the police?"

Kent said, "Yes, I know when she left. I also know why she left, and yes, she was the person who called the police."

Dean almost snarled at his doorman.

"Maybe you would be kind enough to share your knowledge with me."

Kent nodded. "On the first day you were absent, I told Miss Benson that you had gone away, and although she tried to hide it, she was upset. About an hour after the day started, Miss Benson arrived in the foyer shaking and crying. Someone had ripped her shirt in half, and she sported a red mark from a hand on her face. Miss Benson collapsed into my arms, and I held her while she cried. I wanted to call the police, but Miss Benson said that Preston would say she propositioned him, and even though Mrs Yardley wasn't in the room, she would say it was consensual. I gave her a shirt to put on, and she went to the ladies' room to clean up. She was less distressed when she returned but said she would not keep working here."

Dean was shocked. "Mike assaulted Amy?"

Kent shook his head. "No, the bastard tried to rape her, and she was quick enough to knee him in the groin and escape."

Dean put his head in his hands and groaned.

"Dear God, she must hate me. I wrote her a letter explaining what I was doing, but I found it in the drawer." Dean held up the envelope to show Kent.

"Mike didn't give her the letter, so she will believe I abandoned her."

"Maybe if you visit her and try explaining. Take the letter to show her that you didn't abandon her."

Dean nodded.

Later that afternoon, Dean stood with the letter gaping at the woman who answered the door. Lorraine Finney introduced herself to Dean as the homeowner and explained the circumstances that had sent Amy away. She apologised for not knowing where Amy went but suggested he call her. Dean knew that Amy answering his call was a faint hope, but he tried anyway. When his call went to voice mail for the fifth time, Dean felt like throwing the phone against the wall. He had no idea how to contact Amy, and if she didn't answer his calls, he would have nothing. Again, Margot had destroyed his life, and he would never forgive her for that.

CHAPTER 16

The call from Danni Grant came early in the morning, and Amy felt excited to know that not only had her investigator found Lucas, but Danni had sent him a letter for restitution. Danni said that she expected the following communication from Lucas would be through his solicitor, and eventually, the parties would have to get together. For the first time since Dean walked away, Amy felt she was getting her life in order. Bizarrely, Amy was grateful to Dean because if he hadn't folded and gone home to marry the witch, she would not have hit on the idea of seeking restitution from Lucas. If everything went according to plan, she could start at university at the commencement of the year, but until then, she would work all the shifts she could get at the bookshop in town.

Meeting with Lucas and his solicitor made Amy feel queasy, but she knew she had right on her side. She and Lucas agreed, and he had reneged and taken advantage of her; now, he had to pay up. Danni and Amy entered the conference room where Danni's receptionist had placed Lucas and his counsel. The men rose when the women entered the room, and Amy noticed Lucas's expensive suit and watch. He looked the same; Lucas always wore his hair styled, and how he filled out the suit suggested that he had continued his gym sessions.

After they introduced themselves, Danni said, "We all know why we are here, so Mr Blane, I would like to hear what you and your client have decided regarding the restitution of funds to Miss Benson."

"We dispute the need for any restitution regarding the money Miss Benson gave my client."

"Mr Blane, perhaps my client should explain why she paid for Mr McCann's medical qualifications."

Amy stared at Lucas for a moment and then sighed.

"Mr Blane, I do not know what Lucas told you about our agreement, but restitution is due. When Lucas and I had been together as a couple for about three months, college was due to start in less than a month. Lucas suggested a plan that would have us both qualified with few loans. Because he said he could get a job sooner and be paid more than I could with my veterinary qualifications, we decided to get him qualified first, and then he promised to fund my uni course. He not only promised me, but he also promised my Father he would honour his pledge."

"Hmm. Was there anything in writing?"

Danni intervened. "Mr Blane, your client made a contract with Miss Benson, and they shook hands on it. He not only used Miss Benson's money for the university qualifications they agreed upon, but he took advantage. He bought expensive suits and new wheels for his car, which my client paid to be registered. The greatest slap in the face was introducing his fiancé to Amy at the graduation ceremony and buying an expensive engagement ring with Amy's funds. Your client, Mr Blane, is a financial predator with no integrity. Amy deserves to follow her dreams, and as she made your client's life easier without paying student loans, he needs to reciprocate."

Lucas spoke for the first time. "I don't have the one hundred and eighty thousand dollars you seem to think I owe."

Danni said, "I don't think you owe that amount; I know you do. Amy has receipts that track your medical and university bills, but she also kept receipts for rent, clothing, food, utilities and petrol. My paralegal has divided the cost of most of those bills in half, as Amy lived in the flat, too, but the largest of the bills are all on you. Man up, Mr McCann and do the right thing."

"What if I don't pay Amy?"

Danni grinned. "I'll take you to court, and by the time I finish, you'll have a truckload of debt and a reputation as a cheater. Good luck with that."

Lucas asked to talk to his counsel privately, and Danni and Amy left the room. But Danni handed the men copies of Amy's paperwork before she left.

"Lucas and I lived together for close to four years before he cheated, and he hasn't even said hello."

"Maybe he feels guilty even though he doesn't want to pay. The money he has to pay you will impact his fancy life with his new car and flash condo."

When the solicitor called them back into the room, they agreed to pay restitution in monthly repayments. Lucas was to deposit the money into Danni's official account, and she would redistribute it to Amy. Amy was relieved that she and Lucas would never see each other again, but his refusal to acknowledge her hurt her. Did she mean so little to him that he could refuse to greet her?

Five Years Later

As Amy walked across the stage, she beamed with happiness. Five years of hard work resulted in Amy achieving her dream of becoming a vet. When the ceremony finished, Amy rushed to join her family, who had come to see her graduate. Her Mother and Father hugged her, and her mum said, "We are so proud of you. Despite the difficulties you encountered, you've achieved your goal."

Amy's Father wrapped his arm around her shoulders and said, "Let's go and celebrate. I booked a table at Renoir's to enjoy a meal and toast your success."

Natalie, Amy's sister, said, "Gosh, I can't believe you've graduated. When that dick Lucas ripped you off, I thought you would never complete the degree."

"I probably wouldn't have if Danni Grant hadn't fought him for support. The costs are prohibitive, and being saddled with a huge debt that grows yearly is not encouraging."

" Are you looking forward to doing your last practice in the country?"

"Yes. I want to specialise in equine medicine and hope Amaroo has many horses. I know there are cattle farms, so if I'm lucky, the locals still use horses to muster."

Amy's Dad, who had been listening to the conversation, said, "Isn't Amaroo the place that has suddenly become popular?"

Amy nodded. "Yes, it's unexpectedly trendy. Many rich people are building MacMansions there, drawn by the hot springs. In a few years, the newcomers will want shopping malls and fancy restaurants and destroy the town that enticed them for relaxation. But I guess it won't bother me. I have three months with Doc Williams, and then I want to come home and work with Doctor Fletcher before he retires."

Amy set out two days later to begin her last practice with Doctor Williams. She had spoken to the man on the phone, and he seemed fair, but sometimes you didn't know what people were like until you worked for them. Her mind drifted back to Dean, and she wondered what he was doing these days. With the prosecutions of his human relations manager and cousin, it couldn't have been easy to continue in business. The saying no publicity is bad publicity doesn't work with companies dealing with public trusts. Salvaging the reputation of Maddox Industries must have been a difficult task, but Amy didn't regret setting the police on Mike Preston and Robert James. Amy shook her head. She didn't want to think about Dean when she was ready to start a new job.

The vet clinic in Amaroo was an old building, but the equipment was top-notch. What had begun as a quiet country practice had grown as the town grew. Instead of only treating family pets, Amy and Trent Williams treated pocket dogs, large guard dogs and everything in between. Thankfully, Trent set aside a day each week when the only animals he saw at the clinic were emergencies, and he and Amy visited the farms surrounding Amaroo. Amy loved these days because she could treat the stock horses' ailments and talk about horses with the farmers. Trent walked her through the setup for AI because when the time came, he hoped not to be in Amaroo. Trent hadn't discussed his plans with Amy yet because he wanted to see how well she fit into the community and how competent she was in treating the animals in her care. So far, she had passed on all fronts, and as the weeks passed, he knew he had to broach the subject of his holidays. At the end of the day, as they cleaned the surgery, Trent invited Amy for dinner. His wife was an excellent cook, and even if Amy refused, she would at least have a meal she didn't heat in the microwave.

Amy met Susan Williams when she arrived, and she chatted with her about business matters on the phone, but the invitation to dine with her and her husband was a pleasant surprise. The meal was excellent, and the conversation was varied and thought-provoking. Amy loved hearing stories about Amaroo when Trent's Father set up the clinic. Susan cleared the dinner dishes away, and despite Amy offering to help, Susan smiled and declined.

"Trent wants to discuss something with you, and if his proposition appals you, I'd hate to have my dishes broken."

"What an excellent way to open the discussion, Susan. Amy, when you came to work with me, I wondered how you would fit into the community and what your skill level in treating patients would be. You have fitted in well and look like an old hand at treating the animals."

"Ah, thank you."

"As you would be aware, clinics might be open for five and a half days, but animals are not cooperative when injuring themselves or becoming ill. The job you have signed up for is sometimes stressful, but it is a joy at other times. It is relentless. Susan and I have not had a holiday in ten years, and I hoped you might extend your stay for another three months so we can go away, travel a bit and lie on warm tropical beaches."

"Oh, I didn't see that coming. Do you think your clients will trust me to treat their animals?"

"Yes, I do. But it boils down to this: either the townsfolk trust you, or I will close the clinic for three months, and they can travel an hour and a half to the nearest clinic. Will you do it?"

"Only if you tell me that Lexie is not having a holiday. I can do the animals and the inventory, but I can't do everything Lexie does."

Susan sat at the table and smiled at Amy.

"You don't know how welcome the holiday will be. We are grateful that you came to do your last practice with Trent. He doesn't trust easily, but you have the confidence of the patients and my husband. Thank you."

"I will put a notice on the outside and inside doors to alert the clients to the change. It might be worth letting Terry at the Amaroo News know that we will be absent for three months. If I start to notify people now, they have a month to get their heads around the change."

The month flew past, and Amy was the only vet at the Amaroo clinic before she knew it. Being accountable was a big responsibility, and Amy admitted to herself that she felt nervous about the task she had agreed to. Lexie's cheery greeting on the first morning buoyed Amy, and the day started like many others. There were booster shots for regulars and minor ailments for others. Amy suspected that some clients came with their pet's minor ailments to judge Amy's competence, but no one left doubting her ability.

Amy knew the cattle breeders would contact her in a month to source semen straws. Most farmers found it cheaper to breed with artificial insemination than paying a lot of money for a bull who stood around for much of the year. Trent and Amy researched breeders who sold the straws so the farmers could deal with the same breeder as last year or change breeders for a different outcome. Amy was confident that she could do the job of inseminating the cows, but it was time-consuming, and when she began working at the farm, the only animals she would see would be emergencies. Each farm visit would take two days, and Trent had asked them to spread out their breeding time since Amy was the only vet present.

CHAPTER 17

Halfway through her second month, Amy felt elated. All the breeders had cows that preg tested positive, and the clinic ran smoothly. Amy was finishing with the elderly dog of a client when a woman entered the building shouting and screaming. As the elderly dog was the last for the morning, Amy walked into the reception area to find a woman cradling an enormously obese dog, screaming for someone to help.

"Madame, calm yourself. Your hysterics are not helping your dog. Carry him into the examination room, and you can tell me what illness your dog suffers from."

The woman laid the dog on the table, and he lay there, his eyes pleading for help. Amy carried the dog to the scale and gasped at the weight of thirty-five kilos for a dog that she suspected was a Jack Russell. The healthy weight for that breed was between ten and fifteen kilos. Dear God, this stupid woman was feeding her dog to death.

" As a rule, new patients need to fill in paperwork, but as we have bypassed that step, could you tell me your name and when the problem arose?

"I am Margot Dimitrio, and when Teddy woke up this morning, he couldn't move."

"Mrs Dimitrio. How......"

"It's Ms Dimitrio."

Amy gritted her teeth. The woman wore thick makeup and dressed to the nines, sporting gaudy rings and what appeared to be diamond earrings, and she wanted to quibble over titles.

"Ms Dimitrio, how long has the dog been so grossly overweight?"

The woman smiled. "He is a little fat, isn't he?"

"By my calculations, your dog is overweight, between twenty to twenty-five kilos."

Amy tested the dog's responses, as well as his heartbeat and stomach sounds.

"Your dog is not paralysed; he is so fat he can't move. I suspect his heart will fail within a few days. There is so much fat around his heart, lungs and the other organs that the kindest thing to do would be to euthanise the dog."

Ms Dimitrio snarled at Amy. "What type of vet are you when your first method of treatment is to kill the dog? No, find another way."

"Ms Dimitrio, you have spent years feeding this dog so much that his legs don't support him, and he can't move. There is no quick fix to lose weight. What you have spent years doing cannot be undone in a hurry. If you refuse to permit me to euthanise the dog, I will keep him at the clinic for a few weeks, hoping to help him lose weight. Return to the receptionist's desk, fill out the paperwork and ask Lexie for the no-responsibility clause."

"What is a no responsibility clause?"

"It absolves us of responsibility if your dog dies, and considering his level of distress, it wouldn't surprise me if his heart gives out. I am not setting myself up for a lawsuit with you. Sign the form or drive to Braxton, eighty kilometres away."

Amy was generally sympathetic to pet owners when their animals were in distress. Still, she had no patience for a woman who was so self-important that she expected Amy to fix a problem that was years in the making. Amy carried the dog to the cages out the back and began to prepare an IV for the poor animal. Once she had connected the infusion, Amy returned to the front office.

"Ms Dimitrio, the dog is on an IV drip, which contains the nutrients and vitamins he needs to keep him alive without eating. I will keep him for two weeks, assuming he lives that long. If you wish to visit him, you may do so during surgery hours, but if you cause a scene, I will ban you from the premises."

The woman stormed out, and Amy shook her head.

"Lexie, did you get a look at the dog? It's about twenty kilos overweight, and she has the nerve to carry on as though this problem is sudden. It would be kinder to put this animal down. You can see the panic in his eyes; the weight loss will take months of dedicated care."

"Do you think she will visit the dog?"

"I don't know. Some people are so stupid that they shouldn't be allowed to own pets."

Two weeks after the initial consultation, Margot Dimitrio waltzed into the surgery.

"I've come to get my dog."

Lexie felt like rolling her eyes, but her innate professionalism prevented the gesture.

"If you sit, I will let Doctor Benson know you are here."

The woman muttered something that might have been a curse. Still, the surgery was busy today, and Lexi doubted that Amy would inconvenience the other clients by taking time out to explain the ongoing treatment needed for the dog.

"Lexi, will you ask Ms Dimitrio to return after lunch? I need to inform her of the treatment her pet needs, but I don't have time now."

Lexi frowned. "I suspect she will voice her disapproval loudly, but if she causes too much trouble, I'll have one of the men in the waiting room to evict her."

As expected, the woman ranted about being ignored until Bruce Jackson, a regular client with an elderly cocker spaniel, approached her.

"Maám, if you look around, you will see all the clients who booked to see Doctor Benson today. If your dog is kennelled here for treatment, I understand that you are eager to get your pet home. Lexi said there are unique treatments for your dog that Doctor Benson wants to explain, and rather than inconvenience six other customers, the ladies can talk to you after lunch."

"What kind of hick business is this? I am an important community member and shouldn't have to wait."

Lexi was tired of the commotion.

"You are no more important than any of our other clients, and if you don't leave, I will ring Seargent Burke to remove you."

Margot frowned at Lexi, but considering the other clients glared at her, she left. The string of oaths that marked her exit made the others grimace. One lady said, "I never liked that c-word, and I suspect she is no lady despite the clothes and jewellery. What a carry-on."

After lunch, Margot Dimitrio stormed into the clinic.

"I hope you have time to see me now. I might have to report you to your supervisor about your poor attitude."

Amy and Lexi laughed.

"Madame, there is no supervisor. I am the vet on duty, and considering Doctor Williams is on a three-month holiday, I doubt he would be interested in your complaint. Do you want Teddy, or do you want to stand here complaining and swearing? Follow me; he is in the crates in the back."

When Amy opened the crate, the dog wagged his tail. She smiled. "Hey, little Teddy, how are you feeling?"

"Ms Dimitrio, I will release Teddy to you, but you must follow some instructions. First, buy Teddy a warm, comfortable bed and place it, and him, on the porch or the patio or whatever you have that is outdoors and undercover. This distance will overcome the problem of him begging for food when you eat. He can spend all day inside if you wish, but when you prepare food or eat a meal, he needs to go outside. Teddy is to be fed nothing except the mixture, which I will show you how to prepare. I want to see him once a week for a weigh-in. He has lost eight kilos, which has given him enough movement to sit up. If you are strict with his diet, he should be fine. I doubt that he will be running around, even when he has lost all the weight, because I suspect his heart is damaged, and so are his lungs. Bring him back if you are worried, and I will see you in a week. Please make an appointment with Lexi."

The woman appeared to understand Amy's instructions, but she had asked Lexi to give the woman a typed list of instructions, hoping Ms Dimitrio would abide by the rules.

Amy enjoyed the clinic routine, and the community accepted her, understanding that Doctor Williams and Susan deserved a break. The first weigh-in for Teddy was positive, and while Amy hoped the small patient would have lost more than two kilos, she understood that any loss was a move in the right direction. Unfortunately, Amy's optimistic hopes for Teddy crashed when Margot Dimitrio returned Teddy for his second weigh-in. Amy weighed Teddy twice, not believing what she was seeing. The dog had gained three kilos, and Amy shook her head.

"Ms Dimitiro, what have you fed Teddy to make him gain three kilos?"

The woman flushed slightly but tipped her chin defiantly.

"Teddy misses his eggs and bacon at breakfast, so I've fed him a small amount."

"Does he miss being unable to move? Did you see the panic in Teddy's eyes when you brought him in here? His eyes were begging for me to do something, and now you are going to continue feeding your dog to death. I would seize him now, but I will allow the animal control officers to act appropriately. Take Teddy home, but be prepared for Animal Welfare to knock on your door. They will fine you and seize Teddy."

"I won't let anyone take Teddy."

"You won't have a choice. Take that poor little dog home and enjoy your short time with him."

Lexi looked at Amy with sympathy.

"I know how disappointed you are with the woman's actions, but it was always a possibility."

"I know, but I feel like I failed."

CHAPTER 18

The Animal Control officer, Clark Simpson, arrived with a dog carrier one morning. He grinned at Amy and said, "I thought I would have to taser that woman to seize the dog. After she tried to beat me with a magazine, she put on a pitiful, sad look, which was supposed to make me feel sorry for her. I only needed one look at the dog to know that another home is the only chance the little blighter has of living a normal life."

When Clark laid the carrier on the counter, Amy opened it to find the dog in as much distress as he was initially.

"He was here for two weeks and lost seven kilos, and Lexi gave her a list of instructions to follow, but the most important was not to feed him anything more than the measured quantity I specified. He lost another two kilos the first week she returned with the dog. Although I was hoping for more, on the second visit, Teddy gained three kilos. She said he missed his bacon and eggs. What a moron. I assume that, seeing that she feels important, we may have a solicitor's letter floating around sooner rather than later. The woman should be banned from owning another pet unless it's a budgerigar she can't overfeed."

"I can take the little bloke with me, but he needs veterinary care. Would it cause issues if you kept him here?"

"The cages and kennels aren't visible from the waiting room, so as long as we don't advertise that he is here, it should be fine."

A week later, when Amy arrived at the first of the farms she visited on a rotation, the reception was frosty and rude. When Amy asked if the farmhands or the farmers had any problems, Jeff Spencer told her they had trucked the horses with health problems to the vet clinic eighty kilometres away. Amy was confused.

"Why would you truck the horses to Blacktown when you knew I was coming here today?"

The farmer glared at her. "At least we know we get the treatment we paid for if we go there."

Amy frowned. "Have I ever given you second-rate service?"

"Only time will tell."

Amy left the farm feeling confused, but when her reception was the same as that of each of the farms she visited, Amy returned to the clinic confused and upset.

"I don't know what the problem is. The farmers suggested that I had done something that would come to light in the future."

"Farmers are a funny lot, but for them all to have the same comment makes you wonder what has happened?"

"If I've done something wrong, it would be nice if one of them would get brave and tell me what I did."

Lexi nodded, but Amy could tell that she looked concerned.

"The farmers are a worry, but so are our appointment numbers. The clients have cancelled half of the appointments they had booked, and another three or four that had standing appointments have cancelled them also."

Amy looked at the cancellations with concern.

"When I took over, it concerned me that the change of vet might cause a drop-off, but after being here for four months, the locals should be over being nervous about having me treat their pets. I suggest we treat the patients that are still loyal and hope for a return of confidence."

By the end of the week, the client numbers had dwindled to a trickle, and as Amy tried to make sense of the numbers, Lexi brought to her attention a considerable concern.

"Amy, the number of cancellations is concerning, but none of the farmers you did AI for have paid their bills. The suppliers of the straws have sent an invoice marked overdue, and the bills for the straws and your services are still unpaid. I didn't get too concerned when the payments weren't forthcoming because the service was expensive. Maybe the farmers had other expenses they paid first, but it's been a month since you did the preg testing, so they owe a large amount. Should I send out another bill to them all?"

"No, I'll raise the issue during my farm day on Thursday. Are there any bookings for those days?"

"No."

The same chilly reception awaited Amy on Thursday at the first farm she visited. There were no animals for her to check, which was strange. Craig Butcher, the owner of that first farm, sneered at her as she questioned the lack of patients.

"Look, Craig, I have been given the same cold shoulder by the farms I usually service, so if I have done something wrong, I would appreciate it if you would tell me the problem."

The farmer laughed at her. "Think about what you have done, and you'll be able to answer the question yourself."

"I can think of nothing I have done that would make the farmers in the district angry, but one thing I can tell you is that you and your mates owe a stack of money to the clinic, and I am tired of trying to make ends meet with a deficit of more than a hundred thousand dollars."

"Well, sweetheart, get used to it because none of us is paying our bills until after the calves are born, and we can DNA test them."

Amy's mouth dropped open, and her eyes widened.

"So, for some bogus reason, you will bankrupt Doc William's livelihood and leave the locals with no veterinary clinic. Why the hell would you need to DNA test the calves? You know which straws you ordered, so what is the issue?"

"Sure, we know what we ordered, but a little bird told us that you switched the straws with those of a lesser bull and are pocketing the money."

Amy looked at the farmer with amazement.

"So a malicious liar has spread a rumour that you and everyone in this town believe. I have been here for four months, and you think I am the kind of person who would risk this practice and my reputation to pocket a few bucks? When I get to the bottom of this, you and your cronies had better be ready to pay the bill and a hefty late fee. I will not be back. You will have to wait until Doc Williams returns, so I hope you have no urgent cases where time is of the essence because the trip to Blacktown might be the difference between life and death."

As Amy drove away, her anger turned to distress. The drop in numbers made sense because a rumour that she substituted the semen straws with an inferior product had made the rounds of the town. How could she unearth the culprit and make them admit to the lies? When Amy returned to the clinic, the place was empty, except for a long-time client with a dog that appeared to have a broken leg. Amy changed into her scrubs and asked Lexi to help hold the dog while she x-rayed the damaged limb. Once she knew how complex the break was, Amy anaesthetised the dog and prepared to splint the limb.

Amy suggested the woman leave the dog at the clinic and collect it after lunch when the anaesthetic wore off.

"You won't have animal control seize my dog? Please, I'll be more careful, I promise."

Amy frowned at the client. "Of course, I won't. Why would you say that?"

"That rich lady told everyone how you had reported her to Animal Control, and they had taken her dog. She said you would do it to others if we attended here, so most clients travel to Blacktown."

"Mrs Banks, the lady is a liar. I did have animal control seize her dog, but I suppose she didn't tell anyone why. I probably shouldn't share her details, but I will tell you what happened since she wants to destroy the clinic. Ms Dimitrio owns a five-year-old Jack Russell terrier. Those dogs are super active and generally weigh between ten and fifteen kilos. When she brought her dog to us, he weighed thirty-five kilos and couldn't move."

As Amy explained to Mrs Banks what had happened between her and Margot Dimitrio, the woman was shocked and angry that Margot had scared so many clients. She vowed to let all her friends know what happened and would ask them to share the truth with their family and friends.

"If a false rumour can sweep the town, let's see how fast the truth circulates."

"Thank you, Mrs Banks. I appreciate your honesty in telling me what the issue is. I have farmers who believe the rumours someone circulated, and I believe I know who that was now."

Once the woman left, Amy told Lexi about the farmers and the rumour keeping their clients away.

"I could try talking to that baggage, Margot, but that would be a fool's errand. I have a solicitor who would sort out this rubbish. I'll call her and see if she has time to visit for a few days."

After explaining to Danni what was happening in the town that was impacting the business, Amy asked her solicitor to visit and help her sort out the mess.

"If you can wait until next week, I'll clear my calendar for four days. Please don't do anything about the farmers, and with luck, your client may spread the truth as distinct from the lies, but I want to deal with her."

While waiting for the truth to circulate and bring customers, Amy and Lexi conducted a spring clean and a stock-take. Unfortunately, Amy needed to order some items, but the lack of funds prevented that. She hoped the dwindling supplies wouldn't impact her service.

Danni Grant arrived around lunchtime on Tuesday. Business at the clinic was picking up, but the cash flow problem was the most important thing to settle. Amy greeted the woman she held in such high regard and handed her the key to her house.

"Leave your things in the guest bedroom, and I made a cold platter for your lunch. Come back when you're ready, and you can tell me what to do."

During the afternoon, Danni gained as much information as possible regarding the dispute with the farmers and the ongoing problem of circulating rumours caused by Margot Dimitrio.

CHAPTER 19

Danni devised a plan of action now that she knew the problem. Because the distributors selling the sperm straws were becoming agitated about the outstanding bill from the Amaroo Veterinary Clinic, speed was of the essence. Danny contacted each supplier and asked if they would participate in a video conference the day after tomorrow. She explained the issue and why the farmers were unwilling to pay the bill and asked if each dealer would have the paperwork associated with the sale with them.

After organising the dealers to be present, Danni needed to get the farmers to the clinic.

"Do you have e-mail addresses for the farmers?"

Amy nodded. "Yes. Lexi sends bills via e-mail, so we have the addresses of most of our clients."

"Good. I'm going to e-mail those gullible hicks, but I also intend to send a letter. Is there someone who might hand a letter to each of those men? Is there a delivery service of some type?"

"We have a courier; would that do?"

"Yes, that's perfect. See if you can organise the man to meet me in an hour, and I will have the letter to each farmer organised. I'll need a list of the men so that each letter has their name on it, and there can be no suggestion they didn't have the information."

Amy was so glad that she had contacted Danni. The woman was tenacious when supporting her clients, and when this all finished, Amy swore that the cost associated with setting things right would fall directly on Margot Dimitrioi's shoulders.

"What are you putting in the letter?"

"I will tell the farmers they have two choices. The first is to arrive at a meeting here in two days to meet with the sellers or pay the bill now. Anyone not attending the conference will receive legal documents suing them for failure to pay. Now, hurry. I have lots to do before I can send out these notices."

Once she had distributed the emails and paper letters, Danni investigated Margot Dimitrio. The woman was the perpetrator, and Danni wanted to know why the woman felt entitled to destroy Amy and the clinic. Once Danni was satisfied she had learned all she could about Margot, she sent messages inviting her to the clinic or meeting in court. As requested, Danni was reasonably confident the woman would arrive after the farmers left.

Two days later, Amy paced. If the farmers ignored the messages and didn't arrive, she would have to follow through with the threat to sue. Amy couldn't imagine the public relations damage the clinic would sustain if a court case went ahead. The clinic was closed for business today, so the sound of a car pulling into the parking lot buoyed her spirits. Car doors slammed, and Amy realised the farmers had come together, possibly to present a united front. Amy did not attempt to greet the men who suspected her of treacherous dealing, but Danni met them and directed them to the chairs facing the pull-down screen.

"Gentlemen, a rumour circulating in the community has placed the clinic in peril. Instead of giving Doctor Benson the cold shoulder after believing a pack of lies, we could have resolved the issue if you had spoken to her directly. Your refusal to pay for the straws a distributor sent and your refusal to pay for Doctor Benson's services has placed you all in a difficult position. Future orders and services may have to be prepaid. Please bear with me a moment while I place a call."

The farmers shuffled in their chairs, but they all fell silent once they focused on the screen. Danni conducted the session with poise, and by the time the dealers on the other end of the line confirmed each farmer's order, they realised that what Danni and Amy said was true.

They had received the correct straws, but they would have to prepay in the future. Danni thanked the dealers for their time, and once she shut off the call, she rounded on the farmers.

"As your distributor said, you have two weeks to pay for the straws. You need to pay for Doctor Benson's services at the same time. I will deal with the woman who started the rumours, but you all need to tell the truth to the farmers who went to other clinics on your recommendation."

Amy knew as soon as Margot Dimitrio arrived. The shrill voice tweaked a long-ago memory, and Amy frowned as she tried to make sense of the feeling that she recognised the voice. Amy had met with Margot Dimitrio numerous times, and while the woman spent most of her time shouting and swearing, today was the first day the voice stirred ancient memories. Danni popped into the surgery to let Amy know the woman had arrived.

"She has a hot bloke with her; apparently, it's her husband. God knows what a hotty like him sees in a shrew like her. Come and join us."

When Amy entered the waiting room, the couple turned towards her voice, and Amy stopped dead in her tracks.

"Dean?"

"Hello, Amy."

Amy backed away from the couple who stood next to Danni. Her voice stuck in her throat, and she felt light-headed.

"Danni, can you, ah .. I can't.."

Shaking her head, Amy turned and fled. In the room's silence, the sound of an engine and the squeal of tyres made it clear that Amy had left. Dean groaned. He knew Amy was the vet he and Margot were to meet because Margot had ranted and raved about the woman who stole her dog, but he never considered the effect his sudden appearance would have on Amy. Dean ran his hands through his hair.

"Damnation, let's sort out this problem."

"Come into the office so we can sit down while we discuss the problem."

Once they sat, Danni said, "Ms Dimitrio, it has come to my attention that you are trying to sabotage the clinic's viability and damage Doctor Benson's reputation. Is there a valid reason for the malicious rumours you stated, or are you just a horrid person who attacks others for fun?"

Margot lifted her nose in the air and glared at Danni.

"I haven't done anything."

"That denial would have more credibility if we didn't have so many witnesses to your nasty game. Sam Booker, the young farmer from Townsend farm, says that you told him Doctor Benson had swapped the semen straws he and the other farmers had ordered for lower-priced straws from an inferior bull. That information spread quickly, as you had planned, and the refusal of the farmers to pay for the straws and Amy's time has left the clinic with a deficit of eighty thousand dollars. Doctor Benson can't order stock or drugs to treat other patients without that money. Do you want to deny the allegations and call Sam a liar?"

Margot huffed. "One witness, big deal. It's not my fault if some stupid cowboy spreads rumours."

"Your denials mean little. Mrs Banks, a loyal customer, visited with a sick dog and begged Doctor Benson not to have the Animal Control people remove her dog. It seems people are taking their pets to Blacktown Veterinary Clinic because you told people that Miss Benson removed your dog without cause and she would do it to them, too."

"You believe a silly old woman?"

"Ms Dimitrio, we can do this the easy way or the hard way. The easy way involves you admitting to spreading untrue rumours and apologising for that, or I will take you to court to sue you for libel, slander and defamation of character. Believe me when I say that if you take the option where I will see you in court, I will take you to the cleaners. I have mentioned two people who have heard the rumours directly from you, but I can find many more if you want to challenge this in court."

Dean, who had seemed distracted for most of the discussion, said, "For God's sake, Margot, admit your guilt and end this farce."

Margot glared at Dean. "She stole my dog, damn it. "

Lexi, who had been eavesdropping on the people in the office, walked into the room and said, "She is a liar. Ms Dimitrio carried her dog in here, screaming and shouting for someone to fix her dog. I assisted Doctor Benson, but the dog appeared paralysed. Doctor Benson weighed the dog, which is of a breed where ten to fifteen kilos is the average weight, and the dog weighed thirty-five kilos. It wasn't suffering from paralysis; it was so fat it couldn't move. Its heartbeat was irregular, and with the fat around its heart and organs, it looked like the best option for the dog was to euthanase it, but Ms Dimitrio refused permission."

Dean looked at his wife. "Is that all true?"

Margot nodded, so Lexi continued.

"Doctor Benson got permission to try to save the dog and placed him in a crate out the back. Over two weeks, with an IV and no food, he lost seven kilos. Doctor Benson allowed Ms Dimitrio to take the dog home with strict instructions on how to feed the dog. At its first weigh-in, the dog had lost another two kilos, but on the last weigh-in, the dog had gained three kilos. When Doctor Benson queried Ms Dimitrio, she said that Teddy loved his bacon and eggs, and she felt mean not giving him some. It was then she decided to call Animal Control to remove the dog and hopefully give the poor little blighter a chance at a normal life."

Danni said, "I suggest you start writing your letter before I add stupidity to my list of grievances."

Dean shook his head. "You are not only a medalling cow; you are one mean bitch. Write the letter."

As Margot wrote the letter to the editor, under Danni's watchful eye, Dean walked to the waiting room entrance and made a phone call. He seemed pleased with the outcome, and when he returned to the office, he said,

"Margot, I can't imagine the townspeople will be welcoming after you've caused so much grief. I suggest you talk to a real estate agent and move back to live near your parents rather than staying here. I have somewhere else to be, so you can leave when you finish your task."

Danni said, "Can I have a private word, Mr Hunter? Let's step outside."

Dean followed Danni out of the building but faced her and said, "I didn't tell you my last name. How did you know who I am?"

"I know Amy's story of betrayal by two men. The first man, Amy, sought legal help to force him to make restitution so she could go to college, but the other man broke her heart. Please don't mess with her. Except for this last problem caused by your wife, Amy has built a new life."

"Miss Grant, I don't want to mess with her. I want to explain what happened and ask for her forgiveness. My marriage is nothing but a name on a legal document. I have never consummated the marriage, and for the two years of our marriage, Margot and I have lived apart. The call I made before was to start divorce proceedings, and my lawyer advised that we have fulfilled the irreversible breakdown of the marriage clause since we have never lived together. Please, tell me how I can find her."

EPILOGUE

Amy barely made it to the bathroom before she vomited. As she lay on the bathroom floor, her sobs wracked her body, and she cursed herself. The woman's name seemed familiar when they first met, but Amy pushed the feeling aside as a coincidence. When she entered the waiting room and saw Dean standing beside the woman who had caused so much distress, Amy thought she might faint. Dean may have managed to stay cool and calm, but there was no way Amy could deal with him and his wife. Seeing him brought back all the hurt and despair Amy felt after he deserted her, and his presence now tainted this place, which had been a refuge.

How long would it take Danni to finalise the disaster Margot Dimitrio had brought to her door? Stripping off her scrubs, Amy climbed into the shower. She let the hot water run across her face and body and felt the tension leave her. She could do this; she had started a new life before and could do it again. After towling herself, Amy slid into her favourite jeans and a tee shirt. When Danni came home, she might order takeaway food and settle in with a bottle of wine. Amy was eager to discover what had happened and if Danni had solved the problem caused by Margot Dimitrio or if they would have to go to court to settle the issue.

Danni heard the car pull onto the driveway and walked to the door to greet Danni. The shock of seeing Dean at her front door slowed her reaction, and when she belatedly thought about closing the door, Dean pushed against it, and Amy, no match for his strength, relented.

"What the hell do you want?"

"I want to talk to you. I want to explain what happened, and I want you."

Amy scoffed. "You seem to forget you are a married man. How could you have married that vindictive, horrid cow? Was your duty that great that you saddled yourself with a shrew for the rest of your life?"

"Please, Amy, let me explain. If you don't want what I want, I will leave and never contact you again."

The desperation in his eyes touched her heart, and she sighed.

"Grab a seat and begin your big explanation."

Dean's relief was evident, and when he dropped into a seat, he fidgeted for a moment before he began.

"You know that my parents wanted me to marry Margot, but after the cheating and the accident, I couldn't marry a woman I actively hated. After meeting you and having you accept how I looked confirmed my belief that it would be for love, not a duty, when I married. I thought we had resolved the situation, but your call made me realise that I had to clarify that a marriage between Margot and me was not on the cards. I decided to travel home, make my point clear and help cancel the plans that my Mother, Mrs Dimitrio and Margot had made. I wrote you a letter to explain all of that...."

"Stop there. I never got a letter or any explanation of what you were doing except from that piece of filth you are related to. Your cousin told me in graphic detail about your reconciliation with your fiance, the wedding that would happen within days and your Hawaiin honeymoon."

"I promise I wrote you a letter; I still have it at home. I made a mistake trusting Mike because I found the letter in my drawer after returning to my office. When Kent told me what happened to you, I raced around to the house, but Lorraine Finney told me why they were home but couldn't tell me where you went."

Dean continued explaining his trip to visit his parents and what had happened during that trip, and the ache in Amy's heart lessened, but the fact remained he was married to Margot. Dean looked exhausted when he finished his explanation, and Amy nodded her understanding of the plot orchestrated by Margot and acted upon by Mike.'

"I believe what you are saying, but that doesn't explain why you are married to Margot."

"I had told my parents about you, and they were eager to meet you, but I couldn't find you. I didn't know your parents' names or which state you lived in. It was like you didn't exist, and my Mother, in particular, doubted that I had met a girl I wanted to marry. Two years ago, I folded to their pressure and married Margot, but much to my mother's distress, there would never be grandbabies because our marriage is only in name. I have never been intimate with Margot; our finances are separate, and we don't live in the same house. I have already contacted my solicitor to start divorce proceedings. Working on the twelve-month separation to prove that we are incompatible is easy because of the way I conducted our marriage."

"Tell me about your face."

"About three years ago, Dad had a severe heart problem, and the doctors decided that he needed open heart surgery. He was in hospital for a month, and one day, as I left his ward, a bloke in a white coat approached me and told me he could fix my face. I tried to brush him off, but the fellow handed me a card and suggested I visit his burns wards before I made a decision. Long story short, Doctor Mc Cloud did the surgery. The pain was indescribable, and the attending doctors kept me in a medically induced coma for close to a week. Even once the pain lessened, they kept me doped up for much of the time. My face needed antibacterial ointment daily, and the nurses also changed the bandages. When I left the hospital, I had to continue to use the ointment and change the coverings. Because Doctor McCloud removed the skin the other doctors applied, I had to wait for the scabs to fall off before I looked normal."

"It sounds horrific. Are you pleased you went through that procedure?"

"If I had known the pain involved beforehand, I would have run the other way, but I'm happy with the results. We have lots to discuss, but maybe for now, just knowing that I didn't abandon you is what I most want you to understand."

"So what happens now?"

"Amy, I love you. I will always love you, but if you don't feel the same, I will leave and continue my miserable life."

Tears welled in Amy's eyes. "You broke my heart. How do I know you won't do that again?"

Dean sighed. "I guess you don't unless you let me prove it daily for the rest of our lives. What are your plans when you finish here?"

"I'm going home, and I want to buy Doc Earnshaw's clinic and set up a horse refuge."

"If I let you go while I sort out my divorce and business, do you promise not to disappear? I want you, Amy. I want to marry you and have a family with you, and I will propose when the time is right."

"I love you too, and I promise not to disappear."

Dean stood, and for a moment, Amy thought he was going to leave, but when he stood before her, she raised an eyebrow.

"Please, Amy, I know I am married, but can I hug you just this once?"

Feeling Dean's arms wrapped around her, Amy knew she had come home. Whatever difficulties they faced in the future, nothing would compare to the pain and trauma in their past. Amy knew there would be obstacles to overcome, not the least of all the dissolution of his marriage, but she felt hope for their future for the first time since she walked away from this man.

Also by Robyn C Rye

Farnsworth Sisters
Marrying a Rogue
Rescuing Hannah

The Buckingham Sisters
Lady Maggie's Challenge
Layla's Unwanted Husband

The Evans Family
Sometimes Love is not Enough
Still the One
Moving Forward

Standalone
One More Chance
Lady Jayne's Reputation
Third Time's the Charm
Can't Stop Loving You

The Marriage Scam
An Unlikely Match
Searching For You
The Unexpected Suitor
The Lady and the Duke
Starting Over
An Unforgettable Stranger
The Duke's Revenge
The Temporary Wife
Against The Odds
Betrayed
No Good Turn Goes Unpunished
Lady Eloise's Soldier
Lillian's Forbidden Beau
Remember Me
Always Second Best
When One Door Closes
Coming Home to You
Chasing Shadows
Fool Me Once
Deserting Lady Audrey
My Unlikely Saviour
Lies and Deception
A New Beginning
Julia's Second Chance
The Hidden Enemy
The Maiden's Redemption
Miss Elizabeth's Season

www.ingramcontent.com/pod-product-compliance
Lightning Source LLC
Chambersburg PA
CBHW051845130726
47987CB00002B/691